Vacation
Hiro

Vacation Hiro

by
Meg Welch Dendler

SERENITY MOUNTAIN PUBLISHING
Springdale, Arkansas

Published by Serenity Mountain Publishing
Springdale, AR

Vacation Hiro

©2013 by Meg Welch Dendler. All rights reserved.

Printed in the United States of America.

www.megdendler.com

Based on Second Edition, 2019

ISBN: 978-1732380684

Cover art by Lesley Hollinger Vernon.

Cover adapted for Second Edition and hardover by Kelsey Rice.

Photos by Scott and Meg Dendler.

Saber-tooth cat image courtesy of the Indiana State Museum and Historic Sites.

The characters and events in this book
are not based on real events.
Well, maybe a little bit.
But the names have been changed
to protect the innocent.
Sometimes.

As with Book 1, *Why Kimba Saved The World*,
this story is full of real events in the lives of
our cats Kimba and Hiro. You will find photos
of them at the end of many chapters, as well as
photos of other cats and events that sparked my
imagination while writing the story. Of course,
Kimba and Hiro don't really talk to alien cats in
our bathroom mirror. Not that I've ever seen.
Maybe they are just tricky.
You never know with cats.

"One meets his destiny often on the road he takes to avoid it."

French Proverb

Baby Hiro, eyes not open yet, snuggled in the nest in the bathtub with a stuffed mama cat. You can see Kimba's head just under Hiro's front legs.

TABLE OF CONTENTS

So Far In The Series:

Some cats are born on Earth and never know who they really are. Others are sent. They are undercover for their years on Earth. They know who they are. They know that they are not from Earth at all. And they are part of a bigger plan.

When Kimba and Hiro were just tiny babies, only a day or two old, a human found them abandoned in a box. He brought them home. He and his wife fed them from bottles and made a nest for them in a large white bathtub. The humans became Mama and Daddy to the kittens, and the sisters became part of a family that included two human children: Mindy and Leia. There were also three more cats in the house: the pure-black sisters Miss Fatty Cat and Slinky, as well as the war-torn, outdoor wild cat, Buddy. Guarding them all was The Big Black Beast, who barked and nipped and followed Mama around.

When Kimba and Hiro were still just gangly kittens, they discovered they were being watched by aliens. But more shocking, they learned they were aliens too! Through the large mirror in their bathroom nursery, Agent Regalus (their alien cat contact) communicated with them. The sisters learned that all cats are really from another planet. It is the job of a house cat to cohabitate with humans and report back on their actions to the Cats in the Mirror. These reports from cats on Earth to cats in space go on all over the world.

As Kimba and Hiro talked with Regalus through the bathroom mirror, he told them about their heritage of freedom and independence from humans. He gave them a series of missions to complete. The first simply involved rubbing their fur on the humans so the agents could track them throughout the city using mirrors located all over town.

Hiro lost interest in the missions, but Kimba loved them. She was excited to be a part of something big and important. It gave her a sense of adventure and freedom. But once she escaped the house to explore outside, she discovered the world is a big and sometimes scary place.

Then Kimba was enlisted to steal the password to Mama's Facebook page and use it to help coordinate a worldwide cat invasion. Feeling guilty, and knowing she should be faithful and loyal to her cat heritage, Kimba obediently began the mission. But, in the end, she could not follow through. Her love for her human family, and her fears for their safety in a world run by alien cats, won out. She failed to complete the assignment.

After that, Kimba and Hiro agreed to stop all communications with the Cats in the Mirror to keep their humans safe. But the sisters' destiny was too large for them to remain cut off from their feline family forever.

1

SPRING BREAK

Wow! Look at the view, Mama!"

Mindy held up her cell phone so she could get a good picture from the balcony. There were palm trees and beautifully landscaped tropical bushes. Waves from the Atlantic Ocean crashed to shore a short distance away. The breeze blew her long blonde hair in her eyes, so she had to stop and try for the shot again.

Mama and Daddy finished setting down the last of the suitcases and grocery bags. It was enough to last all week. Then they wandered out onto the balcony to let the salty breeze wash over them.

"I love that smell!" Mama said happily. "It smells like vacation."

She leaned on the railing, taking it all in.

Daddy laughed and flopped down on one of the lounge chairs on the balcony of the rental condominium.

"Are you ready for a good Spring Break?" Mama asked Mindy, but the teenager was already totally engrossed in texting her friends. Mama sighed.

Leia wandered out onto the balcony too and immediately gasped in delight. But it wasn't the ocean that had her attention.

"Look, Mama!" Leia squealed, pointing to the sidewalk below. "Cats!"

Everyone stopped and stared at the two cats lying peacefully in the grass below.

"Here, kitty, kitty, kitty," Mama clucked, but neither cat even looked up. "I bet they hear that all the time," she joked.

"Can we get some treats for them at the store later?" Leia asked.

"Sure," Daddy said, "but you are not to touch them in any way, shape, or form. Do you hear me?"

Leia nodded her head quickly and leaned back over the rail, clucking her tongue to try to get the cats' attention.

"Leia?" Daddy said. "Did you hear me?"

"Yeah, yeah, sure, sure," she said.

"I mean it. No touching. They are probably feral cats and might bite a silly girl who is determined to pick them up."

Leia stuck out her bottom lip in an overly dramatic pout and returned to calling for the cats.

Mama watched her for a minute and then sighed again.

"We'd better get unpacked," she said.

Everyone groaned.

"Well, how else are we going to find the bathing suits?"

"Yay!" Leia cheered and ran for the suitcases.

Mindy followed along more slowly, still texting.

Daddy joined Mama at the balcony railing, and

3

they both enjoyed the view for another quiet moment.

"Are you ready for a whole week of fun?" he asked her.

"Absolutely," she said.

They both followed the girls inside to get ready for a trip to the beach.

When all was quiet overhead, Thunder lifted his yellow eyes toward the family's balcony. Assured they were no longer feebly trying to get his attention, the gray-and-silver tabby looked over at his partner. Hurricane met his gaze and nodded slightly. Then she stretched out her front legs, her fur a swirl of black and orange.

That night, when the humans all went to sleep, she would head to the pool deck and make her report in the big bathhouse mirror there. The family had arrived with piles of luggage and food. They were not heading home any time soon. These condos, which were the territory of agents

Thunder and Hurricane, were normally rented out for a solid week. That should give the agents working back on the home front plenty of time.

Hurricane's thoughts were interrupted by the rustling of a nearby bush. A large male cat stepped out of the shadows, his sleek gray fur catching the bright rays of sunshine.

"What are you doing here, Typhoon?" she asked defensively.

"Orders from the high commander," he said matter-of-factly. "They want everyone in the area on full alert."

There was another rustling, and Typhoon's partner, Tsunami, strolled out of the bushes to join him. Her puffy orange fur had bits of grass and leaves stuck in it. She twitched her half-tail, removing a clinging leaf. It was all of her beautiful tail that she had left after a run-in with a beast many years ago. Tsunami stretched out on the grass and attempted to clean her fur.

"Traipsing through the bushes is not really my style," Tsunami said between licks. "But you two have a great place to hide here in all these plants."

Hurricane blinked her eyes slowly in agreement and then looked back up at the balcony. Their directions had been very clear. This was a top-priority mission. The safety and security of future High Council Leaders was involved. The specific details were classified, but in the end, it didn't really matter. Hurricane would obey the high commander. She would do her duty and complete any mission she was given, without question or hesitation.

All four of them would.

The house had been dark for hours, and still no one came. The yard was quiet. The Beast had not returned since he got in the car that morning with the family and all those bags full of clothes.

But Hiro knew, if she just waited patiently enough, Daddy would come home soon. He always came home to her.

Hiro curled up in a tight ball under the bed in Mama and Daddy's room. There was nothing to be scared of. She knew it. But the house was really creepy and quiet in the dark with no people around at all. She sighed and watched the bedroom doorway. Any minute now she would hear the garage door, and he would be there.

Daddy will come home soon, she thought. *Daddy would never leave me alone.*

**Stray cats under the balcony in Cocoa Beach.
Clearly they were agents sent to monitor the family.**

2

EMPTY BED

Hiro awoke with a start. Morning had come. Sunshine streamed through the bedroom window. Peeking out from under the bed, Hiro could see Kimba settling in on the window sill to watch the birds in the backyard.

I must have slept right through Daddy coming home, Hiro thought. *Why didn't he wake me up to get in bed with him? I always sleep on his feet. He must have been so lonely.*

Sliding from under the bed, she stretched her front legs out as far as they could go. Then she arched up her back and kicked out her hind legs, one at a time, flexing her toes to work out the nighttime kinks.

Daddy must have wondered where I was, she thought.

But when she looked up at the bed, it was still neatly made, with all of the fancy pillows piled in place.

"They never came home last night," Kimba said without turning around.

Hiro looked up at her and blinked in the bright light.

"Not at all?" she asked.

"No," Kimba said flatly. "Not Mama or Daddy or the girls. Not even The Big Black Beast."

Hiro didn't know how to respond to such an unheard-of event. The family always came home. Sometimes Mama put on her clickity-clackity shoes and lots of perfume, and she and Daddy were gone until really late, but they always slept in their bed at night. For nearly two years, the sisters had lived there. Daddy had been there every night, without fail. Hiro had slept on his feet and kept him safe.

Where could he be? she wondered.

Then a terrible thought burst into her mind.

"Was there an invasion?" she asked Kimba in horror.

Kimba nodded at the window.

"That's what I'm trying to figure out," she admitted. "I didn't notice anything different from the front windows. It all looks the same, except there were no kids walking to the bus stop this morning."

"No kids?"

"Nope. All quiet. It should be a work and school day, but the neighborhood seems really still. Maybe something did happen."

"Should we check? You know, go and ask?" Hiro almost whispered.

Kimba looked down at her sister sitting on the floor next to the bed. Then she looked at the open bathroom door. There could be answers in the quiet darkness of that room. A Cat in the Mirror could still be watching and waiting.

The sisters did not go into the bathroom any-more unless a human was with them. Even if they never spoke about it, they both knew an agent could be watching through the mirror at any time. Kimba wanted no part of getting caught up in any alien cat invasion plans again.

Choosing her human family over her cat family had been horrible, but necessary. Fortunately, that planned invasion a year ago had fallen apart and never taken place. Since then, neither Kimba nor Hiro wanted anything to do with the Cats in the Mirror. The white cat didn't see any reason to change that. If an invasion had happened, they would find out soon enough. Visiting the bathroom mirror could wait.

"Not yet," Kimba answered. "Let's wait and see what happens."

Kimba jumped down from the window ledge and headed into the kitchen for some breakfast, but Hiro remained hunkered near the bed. Their family would come home soon. Everything would be all right. But the strangeness of it all niggled at her thoughts.

Where are all the neighborhood kids? Where are Mindy and Leia? she wondered. *Where is my family?*

Whoosh. A giant wave sloshed over Mindy and Leia as they squealed with glee. Salt water was beginning to crust up in their hair, but they didn't mind. Tiny fragments of sea shells were sharp beneath their feet, but they didn't mind that either. No school for a week. The Florida sun was warm and bright. Everything was perfect.

Mama and Daddy supervised from the beach, stretched out in lounge chairs under a giant red umbrella. Mama flexed her toes and watched the dried sand fall off in bits.

"Maybe I should get one of those fancy pedicures the condo offers," she wondered aloud.

Daddy chuckled and wiggled the sand off his toes too.

"Maybe I'll join you," he said.

That was the funniest thing Mama had heard in quite a while. She laughed heartily as she grabbed a large bottle of chilled water from the cooler in the sand between their chairs.

"I promise to take pictures to post on Facebook if you do," she teased.

"You can see Kennedy Space Center from here," Daddy said, pointing up the beach and across the water. A tall white building was visible in the distance. "We should take a day and go visit."

"I think the girls have other plans," Mama said, stretching out in the beach chair and closing her eyes.

Daddy shrugged. It didn't hurt to hope for something more than days spent waiting in lines at crowded theme parks.

Another wave crashed into the girls, and their squeals caught his attention. Without bothering Mama, he got up and headed out to join them.

From a few yards away, hidden deep in the undergrowth behind the beach, Hurricane continued her watch. Any moves this family made to return home were to be reported immediately. The high commander had made that perfectly clear. Hurricane and her team had never failed to complete a mission. They would not fail this time either.

3

UNAUTHORIZED CHAT

Hiro couldn't stand the wait any longer. The sun was high in the sky now, and still no one had come home. Everything outside looked normal, except later in the morning Kimba had seen a few children running up and down the sidewalk. Maybe she had been wrong about her days. If it was a school day, why were the children running loose?

As the day wore on, Kimba curled up in her bed high up on Mama's bookshelf. She was not really bothered by the family's absence. But Hiro couldn't possibly sleep. She was tired and crabby and worried and lonely.

And thirsty. Hiro refused to share the water dish in the kitchen near the cat food. Drinking that stale water after other cats had their tongues in it was yucky, and she would have nothing to do with it. Going into the kitchen also meant venturing into Miss Fatty Cat's territory. Hiro avoided dealing with that cranky fat cat as much as she possibly could.

Daddy understood that Hiro needed fresh water, and he always took care of her. In the morning and at bedtime, Daddy would turn on the water in the bathtub so Hiro (and usually Kimba too) could get a nice fresh drink. No one had been around to run that faucet since breakfast yesterday.

How could he forget to give me water? she wondered sadly.

Hiro could go into the bathroom and check to see if there were drips of water left behind from the day before. But that would mean going in without a human. If there was no human in the room, the Cats in the Mirror might try to talk to her again.

Maybe she was overreacting. Was an agent cat really still watching, or had they moved on to monitoring other homes by now? It seemed crazy that anyone would bother with observing them after all of this time.

The sisters had not dared to find out what was going on in the mirror since the day they decided not to be agent cats. But Hiro was getting really thirsty. There might be some water left for her. If she was quiet, even if someone was watching through the mirror, he might not notice her.

She decided that risking the slight chance of being seen in the mirror was better than the icky communal water dish and dealing with Miss Fatty Cat. Hiro tiptoed quietly to the bathroom door. She could see the mirror from there.

Can anyone see me? she wondered.

After gathering her courage, Hiro slunk rapidly across the open expanse of bathroom tile. She leapt into the large bathtub that she and Kimba used to call their nursery and hunkered down along the side. Many happy baby days had been spent in this tub—tussling and playing, unable to escape the high white walls. Now she hoped those walls would hide her from whoever might be watching through the mirror.

After a few minutes of quiet, Hiro felt confident that she was alone. She snuck over to the big silver faucet and reached up high to sniff at the mesh on the underside of it. With one paw hooked over the top of the faucet, she could just balance carefully enough to lick a few droplets of water with her rough tongue.

"Greetings, Hiro." The deep voice echoed through the bathroom.

Hiro froze in fear. If she didn't respond, maybe he would think she hadn't heard him.

"It has been a long time since you have made a report," the voice continued.

A bit of water had gotten stuck on the inside of Hiro's nose, and it made her sneeze.

Snerk.

"Bless you," the voice said.

"Thank you," Hiro responded before she could stop herself.

Oops.

Realizing she couldn't pretend not to hear anymore, Hiro let go of the faucet and looked up at the mirror on the wall over the sink. It was hard to see clearly from her sideways angle, but Hiro could tell immediately it was not Regalus. This cat was thin, like Slinky, but had short, tan, sleek fur with dark-brown ears and markings around his blue eyes. His whiskers were long and black.

"Are you ready to make a report?" the Cat in the Mirror asked.

"About what?" Hiro asked hesitantly.

"Do you know where your humans are?"

"No," she said sadly. "They didn't come home last night like they should have."

"Correct," the cat said. "And from all of the items I saw them packing, they will be gone for a very long time."

Packing? Hiro wondered. *Is that what all of the bags of stuff all over the floor was about?*

"Do you know where they went?" she asked him.

"Our agents in Cocoa Beach, Florida, have confirmed seeing them. The family is playing on the beach and having a wonderful time."

"Daddy is safe?" she asked.

"Very safe. He's having a delightful time with his human children."

That made her feel better, but also a bit sad. Daddy was having fun without her. Did he miss her as much as she missed him?

"When will they be back home again?" she asked.

"Not for many days, I imagine."

"Oh," she sighed. "Where's Regalus?"

"Special Agent Regalus is busy with other matters these days," the Siamese cat said. "I am Special Agent Artemis. I will be your contact for the next missions and reports."

"I won't do any missions," she said firmly. "I need to keep my family safe."

"That is very honorable of you, Hiro," he said, "but there are things beyond your human family that are important. You have other responsibilities.

20

You have a destiny."

"Regalus kept telling us that," she grumbled.

"The facts have not changed. Destiny is tricky. You can't direct it or change it. By its very nature, it is inflexible."

"I guess I just don't understand what my big destiny is. I'm just a plain little black-and-white tuxedo cat living in a normal house with my family."

"Yes," the tan cat said with a devious twinkle in his eye, "that is your cover. It is where you are hiding."

"Hiding?" she said. "Hiding from who?"

Artemis shifted his weight and appeared ready to say something important, but then Hiro heard a loud clunk. The front door clicked open.

Daddy? Hiro thought hopefully.

"Hello, kitties," a female voice called through the house.

The image of Artemis vanished immediately, and Hiro darted under the bed in a flash. From her hiding place, she could hear noises in the kitchen and then the shuffling sound of the big litter box being cleaned out. Water ran at the kitchen sink. Then the delightful sound of cat food pouring into a bowl. Hiro had not eaten since the night before. Her tummy grumbled at the thought.

"Kitty, kitty, kitty," the sing-song voice called. It sounded sort of like Mama, but not really. "Hello, Kimba, how are you today?"

It knows her name? Hiro wondered.

Then footsteps came closer. Hiro saw a pair of white tennis shoes enter the bedroom.

"Hiiirooo?" the woman called out.

It knows MY name?

Watching from under the bed, Hiro saw the white shoes walk into the bathroom and stop at the edge of the tub. Water started running.

"Hiiiirooo, are you thirsty?"

Yes, she was very thirsty, but she was not at all sure about coming out from under the bed with this stranger in the house. As she hesitated, Hiro saw Kimba's feet trot past the bed and into the bathroom. In a swift and agile move, Kimba leapt into the tub. She wasn't about to miss a chance at fresh water right from the tap.

"Here," the woman said, "I'll close up the drain so there's some for Hiro later. Where is that silly cat?"

The water made a splashing sound and then stopped. Gentle lapping noises came from the tub, where Kimba drank to her heart's content. Hiro jealously felt the dryness in her own throat, but she was terrified of this stranger in her bathroom. She stayed hunkered under the bed in fear of what might happen next.

The woman in the white shoes walked back past the bed and out of the room. Moments later, the front door opened and closed again. The deadbolt was thrown back into place with a thunk.

Kimba jumped out of the tub and trotted to the side of the bed, where she could see Hiro hiding.

"You missed a chance at some fresh water, scaredy-cat," she said, crouching down in front of Hiro.

"Who was that, and how did she know our names?"

"That was Grandma, silly," Kimba said. "She's here all the time. Didn't you recognize her?"

"No," Hiro said, a bit embarrassed. She didn't like to come out when anyone unfamiliar was in the house.

"Well, she cleaned out the potty box and gave us some fresh food and water and even ran the faucet in the bathroom just for you. There's some water left behind if you don't mind drinking after me."

Hiro did mind a little, but sharing with Kimba wasn't as bad as when Miss Fatty Cat and Slinky used the bowl too. Reluctantly, Hiro started out from under the bed to get some water. She paused at the door to the bathroom, and Kimba watched her cautiously.

"Are you going in there alone?" she asked.

"If I'm quick, it should be okay," Hiro said, not mentioning the cat she had seen in the mirror just a few minutes before. She was so thirsty, and Kimba would never let her go in if she knew what had happened. "It may be a while before Daddy comes home, and I really need a drink."

"I'll keep watch for you," Kimba said bravely, "and you can run if anyone shows up in the mirror."

Hiro darted into the bathroom, jumped quickly into the tub, and lapped up some of the nice refreshing water left behind when the drain was plugged. Kimba stood guard at the door, watching the mirror intently, but no one appeared. When Hiro was done, the sisters both jumped up on the big bed for a much-needed nap.

From the sofa in the next room, Miss Fatty Cat had listened to it all. She was older and more experienced in the ways of humans. From the size of the suitcases, and the fact that Grandma came to feed them, the fat cat was sure the family would be gone for a long time. She wondered what trouble the kittens would get into with that much time on their paws.

Still very young and gangly Kimba and Hiro,
catching a nap together in Mama's office.

THAWUMP

When Hiro awoke a few hours later, Kimba was gone, and the light through the bedroom window was dim. She listened intently, both radar-like ears turning and shifting in all directions, but there were no sounds to indicate that her family had returned. The TV was quiet. Even the low hum of computers from different rooms was gone. Just silence in the air.

Her tummy grumbled. She was so anxious about getting water earlier that she had forgotten to eat. Hiro glanced toward the bathroom where Daddy always kept a small dish of food and a special litter box just for her.

Daddy.

Her heart ached, missing his furry face. The big bed was cold and lonely without him.

Going into the bathroom for dinner meant chancing another encounter with Artemis, the Siamese Cat in the Mirror. She and Kimba had agreed to avoid those contacts at all times, and she had already broken that rule once. But going into the kitchen for food had its own set of problems.

She was faced with a dilemma. Getting food would mean either risking alien cats or being vulnerable to a thawumping by Miss Fatty Cat.

If Kimba is here, she can help fight off both of them, Hiro thought.

She called out once: "Merow."

Twice: "MEROW!"

But no one answered. A loud grumble from her stomach urged her to decide on her own. She concluded that dealing with Miss Fatty

Cat was easier than taking her chances in the bathroom. For the first time since Daddy had abandoned her, Hiro was forced to leave the bedroom and forage into the kitchen for some food. Her tummy could be denied no longer.

Jumping down from the bed as quietly as she could, Hiro tiptoed to the doorway and peeked into the living room. The sunlight was fading, but Hiro's bright cat eyes could still make out the empty sofa and chairs.

On the alert for Miss Fatty Cat, Hiro swiftly padded across the carpet and to the corner of the kitchen. A quick glance up the stairs to the girls' rooms and around the corner into the kitchen showed no signs of the fat ambushing cat. Hiro was safe, so far.

Another quick dash across the tile floor brought her to the little room that contained the two giant clothes-washing machines, a huge litter box, and the food and water dishes that all four cats were supposed to share.

Normally, the big white door would be shut, and Hiro would need to slink her way through the small swinging cat door at the bottom. If it was left open, The Big Black Beast would sneak in and eat all their food in one gulp. Mama would scold him, and he would look very sorry, but he would do it again the next chance he got.

With The Beast still gone, there was no reason to have the door closed. Mama had left it open, allowing Hiro easy access and a better line of vision to avoid any other cats in the area. She wondered if Mama had done that on purpose.

Positioning herself carefully so she could see the doorway and be ready for an attack, Hiro crunched and munched happily. Finally, with a full tummy, she took a desperate sip or two from the water dish everyone shared. *Yeesh.* Then she made a trip to the litter box, still freshly cleaned by Grandma. Full and content, Hiro strode happily out of the laundry room.

Thawump!

Miss Fatty Cat landed her full and extensive weight on top of Hiro's head. Then, with a satisfied snort, the fat cat stalked back up the stairs.

Hiro, now flat on the floor, sighed. She had let her guard down, as she had so many times before, and taken the pounce she should have seen coming.

What is it about a full belly that makes me forget to watch out?

Sadly, Hiro picked herself up and shook her head to clear the fuzziness left behind from the squashing. Then she wandered quietly back toward the bedroom. There was no hurry now. Once Miss Fatty Cat had done her worst, she left you alone. Glancing toward Mama's office, Hiro could see Kimba in her usual spot, sound asleep up high on the bookshelf surrounded by dozens of stuffed animals.

The lamp in Mama's office suddenly clicked on, casting a soft glow across the living room.

"That means they will be gone for a long time," Miss Fatty Cat said, looking down through the banister spokes at Hiro from half-way up the stairs.

"How do you know?" Hiro asked.

"This isn't the first time the family has gone

31

on vacation. It's just the first time for you. When they set the lights to go on and off, and Grandma comes to take care of us, that means they will be gone for many, many days."

Without waiting for a response, Miss Fatty Cat pulled her way up the rest of the stairs to spend the night on Leia's bed, even if she wasn't there to share it.

Many, many days, Hiro thought.

Daddy was too far away. Artemis had said Daddy was at the beach. Hiro wasn't exactly sure what a beach was. She just knew he wasn't with her. She slunk back into the bedroom and curled up under the bed alone. With a deep sigh, she tried to go back to sleep to make the time pass faster.

Artemis watched Hiro return and tuck in under the bed. He had hoped she would come into the bathroom for her food and litter box, like she normally did when the humans were around. That would allow him a perfect opportunity to talk with her and help her understand how important she was to cats across the universe.

Miss Fatty Cat, giving a good thawumping to Bolt.

5

FAMILY HISTORY

Hiro slept restlessly under the bed that night. Even though the temperature in the house was pretty much the same all year round, it felt extra cold without the warmth of Daddy to cuddle up to. The carpeted floor was soft enough, but not as soft as the big bed. She just couldn't face sleeping up there alone. It felt safer to be hidden.

When daylight came, she jumped up on the bed for a stretch and her morning bath. She licked the dust and hairs off her back and cleaned carefully between each toe. Then it was time for breakfast, and a new decision lay ahead.

There was plenty of food in the kitchen. The shared water bowl and litter box were there too. But venturing out to that area yesterday had resulted in a solid pouncing from Miss Fatty Cat. Hiro preferred to avoid that today.

The solution was simple. Go into Mama and Daddy's bathroom where she had her own food and litter box that Daddy had set up to protect her from the fat cat. What he didn't know was there were things in the bathroom that Hiro needed shelter from too.

Normally, Daddy or Mama was around in the morning to shield Hiro from making contact with the Cats in the Mirror. Their attempt to talk with her again made it clear that someone from headquarters was still watching and waiting, even if it had been months since Hiro or Kimba had been alone in the bathroom without a human.

The Cats in the Mirror would never show themselves if there were any chance of a human seeing them. So for many months, all through

Christmas when the family brought a huge tree right into the house and wouldn't let the cats climb it, there had been no conversations with Regalus or any other alien cat. Life had gone back to being simple and carefree.

Now, with the humans gone, every day and night was filled with chances for an agent cat to appear in the mirror. There wasn't any temptation to get involved with the aliens' plots and plans, but Artemis had hinted at something that left Hiro with big unanswered questions. He had said the sisters were "hiding." That sounded like something she should know more about.

What would I have to hide from, except that old, fat, dumb cat? she wondered.

Just to have a conversation with Artemis did not mean she was agreeing to be part of their plans. She wouldn't even have to call out for him. She could just go into the bathroom and get her breakfast (and be safe from attack by Miss Fatty Cat). If Artemis showed up, she could ask him about the hiding thing. If there was something scary to be worried about, it would be best to know so she could tell Kimba and they could be careful.

Leisurely, without fuss or bother, Hiro slid off the bed and sauntered into the bathroom, just like it was any other day. She quickly visited the litter box, glad it had a cover so she had some privacy. Then she jumped up on the ledge of the sink where a bowl of dry cat food waited for her.

She took a few bites, the crunches echoing off the tile walls of the empty bathroom, before she heard the voice.

"Greetings, Hiro," he said calmly.

She finished her bite and sat up to face his image in the mirror.

"Good morning, Artemis," she answered.

"I'm glad you are not afraid to come into the bathroom without the human male," he continued. "You really don't have anything to fear from me. I'm only here to monitor and help you."

"I don't really think I need any help. Thanks all the same," Hiro said.

"Every cat on Earth needs help," Artemis said.

"A cat who is not free to embrace his or her destiny, especially a special cat like you, needs extra help every day."

"What's so special about me?" she wondered. "I'm just like any other house cat in the world."

"Part of that is true," he admitted, "you are like many other house cats. But you have a heritage and a plan for your life that is far beyond any of that. Special Agent Regalus had started to explain that to you before you and your sister broke off contact with us."

"He used to talk about our destiny all the time, but he never explained what it is or why it is important. It doesn't really matter anyhow. Kimba and I are quite happy where we are right now."

"Does Kimba know you have made contact with me?" Artemis asked, lowering his dark whiskers.

"No," Hiro admitted. "I didn't tell her. She wouldn't like it."

"You are correct. She would not like it. So let's just keep our chats between us for now."

That sounded a little suspicious to Hiro, but

she wasn't about to agree to do anything for this cat. There was no danger in just talking. Maybe she could find out some more about where she and Kimba came from. There was certainly not much else to do in the house all day and night without a human to play with.

"Okay," she agreed. "I won't tell her, for now."

"Good."

"Will you tell me who I am hiding from?"

Artemis paused at this request. He hadn't really meant to open that can of worms just yet, but maybe it was exactly what the black-and-white cat needed to hear. He only had a few days to convince her that her loyalties needed to shift from the humans to her cat family. Understanding who she really is might just do the trick.

"Yes," he blinked slowly, "but we will need to start with a bit of history of your family first."

"My family has a history?" Hiro marveled.

"Oh yes, a very long and proud and honorable history. Hiro, you are what the humans call royalty."

Hiro had to think about that word for a bit. *Royalty?*

It reminded her of something the family had watched on TV while she was stretched out on the back of the sofa. There was a big wedding in another country with lots of men in red uniforms and a huge church and carriages. Mama had explained to the girls about the bride with the long dark hair. She was joining the royal family, and she would probably be the queen someday.

Leia knew about some of the history of that country from a class she had taken at school. Mindy knew even more about wars and battles that had been fought hundreds of years ago over who got to be in charge and who was king or queen. Hiro could remember thinking it was all a bit odd.

Artemis watched closely. Hiro's whiskers twitched as she considered this new information.

"I have seen things on the TV about royal families that Mama says are far away across the ocean," she finally said. "Mama says we don't have royal families in America."

"This is true," Artemis admitted. "You probably saw the wedding of Prince William of England. But where you are from, your family is just as important as the ones you watched on television. Actually, even more important."

Hiro blinked in response. She didn't know the name of the man in the bright-red jacket. She had only been half paying attention. It didn't seem to have anything to do with her own life, until now.

Royalty? she wondered. *Kimba and I are royalty?* It was all very confusing.

Artemis hesitated. Hiro's tail had begun to swish, and little spots along her back twitched in agitation, like someone was poking her with a stick. She had no intention of getting tangled up in a game of chase-the-tail right now, but sometimes her body didn't cooperate.

Noticing her anxiety, Artemis thought the better of continuing to load her mind with new information. He had some time to be patient.

"That may be enough for you to process right now," he said. "Just take some time to consider what it means to you that you are part of a vitally

41

important family. You are part of a family that needs you to be ready to take your rightful place. You are royalty, and there is no getting around it. It is your destiny."

Hiro stared blankly at the mirror, not sure how to respond. The tic in her back jumped, and her tail thrashed rhythmically from side to side.

"Relax. Get a good nap. After the grandmother has come and gone today, and you are sure the other cats are asleep, come back and we will talk some more about your family."

Artemis's image faded from the mirror, and Hiro was left alone in the bathroom.

How is this possible? she wondered. *I'm just a kitten that Daddy found abandoned in a box.*

The thought that a cat might still be watching her through the mirror was unnerving, so Hiro jumped down and staggered out into the bedroom. For a moment, she worried that Kimba might have been listening to the conversation. But there was no one around. She jumped back onto the bed and curled up into the smallest ball she could.

Normally, when something confusing like this happened, she could turn to her sister for help. Kimba was usually the one getting into messes. Hiro didn't have much personal experience coping with perplexing information.

Hiro had thought all of their dealings with the Cats in the Mirror were over. She never expected to talk to one of them again. Now, not only was she talking with one of them, but she was hiding it from her sister. And the agent cat was full of really startling revelations about how she and Kimba were royalty. All of that talk about grand destinies was back.

We decided to protect our family, Hiro reminded herself. *We are going to keep them safe, no matter what.*

But then she had a somber thought. Maybe the humans didn't need cats to keep them safe. Daddy had gone away, far away for a long time, and didn't seem to need her help now. She was the one who needed him. There was no one to give her kisses and hugs and cuddle with her at night. Hiro sighed and tucked her face under her front leg and into her belly as tightly as she could.

Daddy.

When Hiro left the room, Artemis looked away from the mirror and pressed the large red button next to his computer screen. It might be a while before the high commander could get back to him, but he knew she would want an update.

Hiro had become visibly anxious over the smallest and simplest piece of information he had to share. Finding out that she is a royal cat was only the tip of the iceberg. How would she respond to the rest of what he had planned for her week-long vacation from the human male?

It was vital he gain her trust and that she understand her place in the world. Having the humans away for a few days was the perfect opportunity. Now he would just have to tread slowly and carefully. If he scared her away from the mirror again, she might never return.

Artemis knew he could not fail. The future of

these sisters, and the future of his own ship, rested on what came next.

Glancing back at the sleeping form of Hiro on the bed just outside the bathroom door, the Siamese cat sighed deeply.

Patience, he thought. *I must have patience.*

Hiro, draped over the sofa.

6

WARRIOR COUSINS

Mama tried to find a quiet place so she could hear Grandma on the other end of the phone line. Plugging her ear and shouting was as close as she could get.

"Everything okay there?" she asked.

"Yes," Grandma said. "I went by again today and cleaned the boxes and ran water in the bathtub like you said to. Kimba followed me around the whole time, but I never saw Hiro or the other cats inside. Buddy showed up for his food on the porch as I was leaving, so he's all set."

"Good, good," Mama said, hoping she had heard it all correctly over the din of the music and the delighted, screaming children. "I'm sure they are all fine and just hid when they heard you come in. They do that even when we are home."

"True," Grandma said. "I'm not sure I've ever had more than a glimpse of Slinky."

"Just make sure no one is shut up in a bedroom or something, and they will all make it through until we get back on Sunday."

"Okay," she said. "Are you having fun?"

"Of course! We are heading over to see 'Lion King Live,' and a guy in the park just made up a song about Leia and sang it over the loud speaker. I wish I'd had the video camera!"

Several children ran by, shrieking and waving their arms.

"Sounds great," Grandma said, grateful she was in her nice peaceful house instead. "I'll check in with you again in a few days. Have fun!"

"Okay, bye!"

Mama flipped her cell phone closed and

looked around to see where the rest of the family had gone. Daddy was having his picture taken with Goofy, and Mindy and Leia were sitting on a park bench nearby eating giant ice cream cones. Each of them was in a battle with the sun to devour the treats before they melted down their arms. Mama smiled and joined the girls on the bench.

"Want a bite?" Mindy offered.

"No." Mama laughed. "Not after that cinnamon roll the size of my head I ate this morning."

Daddy flopped down on the park bench next to her.

"What a day!" He took a long swig from a bottle of water. "Was that your mom on the phone?"

"Yeah. She says everything looks fine, but the only cat she has actually seen is Kimba."

"Hiro's probably hiding under our bed. I hope Miss Fatty Cat isn't giving her too hard a time. I wonder where she's sleeping without me there."

Daddy gazed off into the distance, worry furrowing his eyebrows.

"She'll be just fine." Mama laughed. "How many times have we gone on vacation and left cats at home? No big deal. I'm mostly worried about Buddy showing up at the right time before a possum or a stray cat gets his dinner."

"Buddy's tough. He'll be fine. We've just never left Hiro alone for even one night. She must be so lonely and scared."

Daddy shifted uncomfortably in his seat. He wished Hiro could talk on the phone too so he could make sure she was okay and tell her he would be back soon. He had tried to explain the vacation to her before the family left, but he was pretty sure she had not understood.

"She'll be fine," Mama assured him. "Now let's get into the theater so we can find good seats."

Grandma had come and gone again that day, but Hiro still refused to come out when she was there. The minute she heard the door click, Hiro had darted back under the bed and wedged

49

herself in against the wall. The sad cat had heard Grandma calling for her, but she knew she probably wouldn't bend down to look under the bed. That would take a lot of effort for such an old human.

Once she heard the deadbolt click back into place and was sure that Grandma was gone, Hiro slipped out from under the bed. She hesitated at the edge of the carpet that marked the end of the bedroom and the start of the hard tile bathroom floor. Water was waiting for her, but so was Artemis or some other agent cat.

The Cat in the Mirror was prepared to tell her about her family and their royal heritage. Questions tickled around inside her head. Part of her was scared of what he might have to say. The other part was still a curious kitten who couldn't stand not knowing something so important. She had to find out more or it would drive her crazy!

She listened for a moment, her black ears turning from side to side, wondering where Kimba was. Hiro had still not told her anything about making contact with Artemis. Her sister would not be happy about it. She was sure of that.

When Grandma was there, Kimba had followed her into the bathroom to get a drink of fresh water. She had probably gone into the kitchen after that. Delaying her trip into the bathroom for a moment, Hiro trotted over to the bedroom door and peeked out. There were no other cats to be seen.

She couldn't risk being caught talking to Artemis just yet. Kimba would put a stop to it, and Hiro really needed to hear what he had to say.

Tiptoeing farther out into the house, Hiro finally found Kimba curled up on a dining room chair. Her sister looked up at her with sleepy eyes.

"Time for a nap?" Hiro asked.

"Mmm," Kimba murmured. "All full of food and water and ready to snooze."

She tucked her nose in under her front leg and sighed deeply. Hiro knew that in moments Kimba would be oblivious to anything but her dreams.

As she walked back past Mama's office,

51

Hiro could hear deep snores coming from underneath the sofa. Miss Fatty Cat was already asleep. Slinky wouldn't come downstairs until dark, but Hiro wasn't too worried about her anyhow. She never came near the grown-ups' bedroom.

Assured the coast was clear, Hiro trotted quickly back to the bedroom and right into the bathroom. Leaping nimbly into the tub to get a drink of water first, Hiro finally jumped up onto the counter. She sat up straight and tall.

"Artemis?" she called out. "Are you there?"

The image of the Siamese cat appeared in the mirror. His bright-blue eyes were already focused on her.

"Greetings. Has the human grandmother gone away?"

"Yes, she's gone, and everyone is sleeping now."

He waited, watching her closely.

"Um, you said you would tell me more about my cat family. About how I have a royal destiny."

"Are you ready to hear all of that now?"

"Yes," she answered eagerly.

"Once you know some things, you can never *unknow* them."

Hiro tipped her head slightly, not sure what he meant.

"Once you know who you really are and why your destiny is so important, you may not be able to just sit back and live the life you have enjoyed so far. Sleeping under a bed all day and cuddling with a human male might lose its appeal."

Hiro doubted that. What could possibly be better than her life with Daddy?

"I'm still ready to hear it," she assured him.

"All right, then. Let me give you a little history first. You need to understand who you are related to and where you actually come from. Your feline ancestors have lived in the universe for millions of years. Far longer than human beings.

"The planet your family originally came from is so far away among the stars that even the most powerful Earth telescopes cannot see it.

Humans do not have a name for it, but it is rather like Earth with blue skies and air we can breathe. That's why our ancestors settled on your planet millions of years ago."

"Did we have to leave our planet?" Hiro asked. "Was something wrong?"

"We did not have to, but the bravest among us chose to set out to explore the universe. Cats are inclined to be adventurous. Some more than others. The earliest ships to leave our planet were filled with those most thrill-seeking cats. They were the warriors among us. Their large, sharp fang teeth gave them the power to hunt and eat and conquer the most massive beasts on Earth."

Hiro thought about her own fang teeth. She was pretty sure they would not get her very far in the wild world she had seen on Mama's nature specials on TV.

Sensing her thoughts, Artemis explained. "The first cats were not small and delicate, like you and I are. They were enormous, fearsome beasts. More like a lion or a tiger than either of us. Like this," he said. After clicking a few buttons, an image appeared next to him in the mirror.

Hiro's eyes widened.

"I've never seen anything like that!" she gasped.

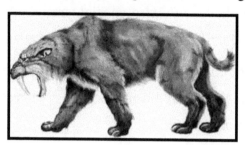

"Of course not, except maybe on TV in a historical special. Groups of cats like this and their distant cousins, who are really more like kangaroos than what are now cat-like creatures, made several landings on Earth going back seventy-two million years."

Hiro couldn't quite process what a million years was, much less seventy-two million, but she knew it was a really, really long time.

"There were more than thirty-five different kinds of prehistoric cats like this one. They came in all shapes and sizes—from eight hundred pounds to just like you and me. This is a picture of one the humans called a saber-tooth cat, or more scientifically *Smilodon Fatalis*."

"He doesn't look very smiley to me," Hiro said in awe.

"No, it means 'deadly knife tooth,' though he does have an extra-special smile," Artemis remarked with pride in his ancestral cousin.

Deadly knives, indeed, Hiro thought. *He looks like he has a pair of Mama's kitchen choppers sticking out of his mouth.*

"Our ancestors didn't have any way to keep in touch. Earth was sort of a dropping ground for the super-fanged cats to get away from it all and be wild. Once humans came on the scene thousands of years ago, the last of the saber-toothed cats on Earth became extinct. It was a hard time.

"The Ice Age ended, and lots of the big animals they ate as food died off. They also had to compete with the human beings that were taking over the Earth in the warmer temperatures. The adventuresome saber-toothed cats who were still on the ships flew away and chose other planets where they could run the show without humans to bother with."

"Cats like that are still around the universe

somewhere?" Hiro asked, her whiskers flexing and twitching.

"Oh yes, but we don't interact with them much. They have their own plans and agendas. It's all about the thrill of living wild. The other groups of cats to come to Earth near the end of the saber's time there were smaller but just as fearsome and still the biggest predators on Earth. They spread themselves out nicely over all of the continents the planet had to offer. Tigers and lions and panthers and all kinds of other cousins, they took over the vast jungles and grasslands and enjoyed being the top of the food chain for thousands of years."

Hiro had seen many movies and TV shows about lions and tigers. The girls loved to watch *The Lion King,* even though it made them cry when Mufasa dies. Mama watched specials about Africa and endangered animals all the time.

Endangered, Hiro thought. *That's the word they always seem to use for those wild big cats.*

"Wild cats seem to have a really hard, danger-ous life," she said solemnly. "Why would they

57

choose to live like that?"

"Things used to be in balance," Artemis said sadly. "Our glorious cousins used to live in harmony with the land around them, hunting only what they needed to live. Early humans were much like that too. Things have changed."

"Can't you save them?" she asked. "Can't they just pick up and go back where they came from if they want to?"

"We have lost touch with them," he admitted. "Out here in the universe, they have their own ships and forms of leadership that don't include us. The policy is that the original settlers knew the risks and went anyhow. Now, just like you only a few months ago, those wild cats know nothing about their heritage or where they come from. The old stories have been lost in a struggle to survive. Just like the saber-tooths, their ancestors still on traveling ships have found other more hospitable planets and left the ones on Earth to fend for themselves."

"But when did cats like us come to Earth? We are not much like those lions and tigers I see on

TV."

"Even before our lion and tiger cousins started to come to Earth for adventures, about two million years ago, smaller wild cats, more like us, were arriving too. But over time they took on a different role. Our ancestors' job became to make contact with the humans and study them.

"We selected one of the most advanced and thriving communities on the planet, in Egypt, near the Nile River, and worked our way into the humans' lives. We hunted and killed the bothersome small pests that tried to eat their stored food. And we showed off a bit by hunting deadly cobra snakes too."

"They must have loved us for that," Hiro imagined.

"They *worshiped* us," Artemis said, sitting up tall and pursing his mouth so his black whiskers stood out rigidly. "Those humans seemed to understand how special their cats were. Cats were treated as gods, honored, and even given special funerals just like the humans. I am named for the cat Artemis, a special goddess of the moon and the fertility of the earth. They thought our eyes moved like the phases of the moon. Cats were treasured." But then Artemis shifted uncomfortably, and his whiskers dropped.

"Over time, that changed as well. Other religions took over, and cat worship was seen as a very bad thing. It made humans think of witchcraft and evil. Those were dark years on Earth, and we almost gave up on it altogether. But soon cats learned to live side by side with the people again. While our large cousins have mostly been at odds with the humans for food and land, we small cats have become an important part of human life.

"Cats like us are the only ones still attempting to settle and make advances on Earth. All of the other ships have gone away to find some place more welcoming. We live with the humans, instead of being shoved out by them. People see us as cute and manageable. Because we are not fearsome, we are allowed to live with them in harmony. But that could change at any time, just like it did for our beautiful cousins."

"Is that why you want to invade and take over?" Hiro asked.

Artemis tipped his head slightly and then looked off to the side, like Regalus used to do. Someone else was in the room with him that Hiro could not see. Remembering those conversations with Regalus made her ears tingle. It reminded her that she and Kimba had agreed never to talk to the Cats in the Mirror again. Her tail thrashed, and her back twitched twice involuntarily. Trying to remain calm and get an answer from him, Hiro swallowed twice and took a deep breath.

Noticing her reaction, Artemis changed his mind about going further today. He needed her excited, but not suspicious or upset.

"That's enough for now," he said firmly. "You must be tired and missing your human. Why don't you get a nap, and we can talk more tomorrow."

"But I feel like you haven't explained much of anything about my family and why it is all so important," Hiro whined.

"I know, but we have time. I can see that

this new information is making you agitated. Take a while to think about it all. Sleep on it. We cats need our sleep so we are always ready for whatever adventure may come our way. Never neglect your sleep. Sleep is the essence of being a cat. Once you have had a nap, we can talk again."

With that, Artemis's image faded in the mirror and Hiro sighed. He was right. That was a lot of information to process, and she was feeling pretty aggravated and sleepy.

Trotting quickly from the room, headed for bed, Hiro was suddenly faced with a very pink-eared Kimba, who had been listening from outside the door.

"Have you lost your mind?" she whispered.

Kimba, showing off her "knife teeth" too.

7

BUSTED

Kimba glared at her sister, who was now standing in the doorway, frozen in terror. Hiro was never very good at confrontations. Running away from them was always her first choice. But there was no way to avoid the puffy tail and narrow eyes of Kimba today.

Regaining her composure, Hiro tried to saunter calmly from the bathroom so Artemis wouldn't notice anything unusual, in case he was still watching. Once she rounded the corner out of his sight, she sat down and faced her angry sister.

Kimba was in such a rage, she could barely speak. Her nose and ears were a brighter pink than Hiro had ever seen, and her bottlebrush tail thrashed like a snake caught in a trap.

"What are you doing?" Kimba hissed.

Hiro sighed. She hadn't meant to break the rule. She knew why it was important. She understood why Kimba was so angry. They had agreed to stay clear of the Cats in the Mirror at all costs to protect the family. Hiro had broken that trust.

"I just went in to get a drink of water after Grandma came, and he started talking to me. I pretended not to hear, but he tricked me," she answered in hushed tones.

"Why didn't you just go to the kitchen and use that water bowl?"

"I tried that earlier. Miss Fatty Cat jumped me," she admitted. "I didn't think there would be an agent at the mirror watching every second. It's been so long since we made any contact. I thought it would be safe."

Kimba relaxed her posture a bit, and her fur began to settle, but her pupils were still large and black.

"Who is he? What did he want from you?" she asked. "Did he try to talk you into a mission?"

"His name is Artemis, and he didn't talk about any missions. He just wanted to tell me more about where we come from and our family, and all that stuff Regalus would never talk about."

Kimba glanced back toward the bathroom. Curiosity is a dangerous thing for anyone, but especially for a cat. The sisters had never had an answer for one of their questions about their cat family, even though it was supposed to be very important information. Kimba had planned on just scolding her sister and telling her to stay out of the bathroom until the family came back, but now she had to know more.

"What did he say?"

Hiro shared what she could remember about the saber-toothed cats and other warrior cats who came to Earth for adventure. Their huge fangs and how much trouble they had getting along with humans intrigued Kimba.

"I heard the last part," she admitted, "about the cats like us. But that's something Regalus already told us. Our job is to live with the humans and monitor them."

"Artemis said that was enough to say for now, but he told me one other thing."

Hiro hesitated. So far she had made it sound like this was the first time she had talked with Artemis. Maybe Kimba would think it was just information he had shared before she started eavesdropping.

"What?" Kimba asked, agitated to be left hanging.

"He said we are royalty," she whispered.

"Royalty?"

Kimba wasn't quite sure what that word meant, so it didn't help.

"Yes, like the people in that big, fancy wedding we saw on TV with all the carriages and soldiers and thousands of people waving in the streets."

"People stand in the streets to wave at our cat family?" she wondered.

"Maybe back where we come from," Hiro suggested. "Other cats, I mean, not people."

Kimba blinked slowly. *Of course, obviously not people.*

"He also said that we are hiding here with this family."

"Hiding from what?"

"Or who?" Hiro added. "He hasn't told me more about that yet."

Kimba hunkered down. Regalus had never mentioned anything about the sisters needing to hide out. That sounded like there was danger involved. She remembered hiding in the bushes that terrible day she had ventured outside on a mission from the Cat in the Mirror.

The only reason to hide is because you are scared something will hurt you.

"He wants me to come back and talk to him again," Hiro said.

"I heard."

Kimba was torn. When she first heard Hiro talking in the bathroom, she had been furious and set on putting a stop to it. Now she was not so sure. Knowing what they were hiding from could be important.

"He didn't ask you to do anything that might put the family in danger? Any invasions?" Kimba asked.

"No, nothing like that at all."

"Okay, then you should go back when he said to and try to find out everything you can."

Hiro nodded.

"Do you want to come with me next time?"

Kimba's ears and nose flushed pink again as she thought about it, and the fur on her back rose a bit in distress. She was desperate to know more about her cat family and what danger she and Hiro could be in, but she wanted nothing to do with sitting on that counter and finding out.

"No," she said finally, "let them think it's just you. They don't really trust me much anyhow.

Maybe they will tell you more if I'm not there."

"You could hide around the corner, like you did today, so you can still hear," Hiro suggested.

"Good idea. Then if he tries to get tricky, I can be around to help."

"He's not going to get me to do anything that would hurt Daddy," she said.

"Not on purpose," Kimba admitted. "But they can wiggle it around so you don't know what you are doing until it is too late. Trust me on that one."

Hiro nodded. She would never forgive herself if she did something to hurt Daddy. Kimba would guard against that.

Realizing she had not done what Artemis told her to, Hiro glanced nervously over at the big bed.

"He told me to go take a nap. He might still be watching."

"Then get up where he can see you and do it," Kimba encouraged her.

"How am I supposed to sleep with him watching?"

"Just curl up with your back to him, and try

not to think about it."

With that, Kimba snuck back out of the bedroom. Hiro hesitantly jumped up on the end of the bed where she could see part of the bathroom mirror through the open door. Refusing to even glance in that direction, Hiro slowly turned around twice and then curled up as tightly as she could, her back to the mirror.

Hiro was sad Kimba had caught her, but it was probably for the best in the end. The sisters did not keep secrets from each other, and Kimba would have been really furious to find out later. There was no way Hiro could have learned about their family and not shared it eventually. No matter how much the two of them loved their humans, they were still sisters. They stuck together, no matter what. Now if she could just manage to nap with Artemis spying on her.

Despite her worries, she dropped off to sleep in a second.

8

ARTEMIS AND HURRICANE

Be still, Hiro, or you're going to fall over!" Leia said as she pushed the toy stroller off the kitchen tile floor and onto the deep brown carpet of the living room.

Next to her, Hiro saw Kimba lounging in another stroller. Her favorite toy—a long leopard tail-like thing—was tucked in next to her. Then they both began to glide as Leia pushed them slowly around the room.

Daddy laughed as the girl marched the sisters in front of the TV.

"How did you get them in those strollers?" he asked.

"They wanted to," she said.

Daddy looked suspicious.

"No, really!" Leia said in her own defense. "I had the strollers open and was planning to put my dolls in them, but then Hiro jumped in one, and Kimba jumped in the other. They like riding around in them."

To prove Leia's point, Kimba yawned dramatically and curled up a bit more in the tight confines of the stroller seat.

Yes, I do love to be pushed around in this toy, Hiro thought. *It's all cozy, and I fit in just right.*

She looked over at Daddy and saw him smiling his special just-for-Hiro smile. It was almost enough to make her jump out of the stroller and onto the sofa with him.

What's more comfortable, she wondered, *the stroller or Daddy's lap?*

A deep purr rumbled up from her throat. The lap was the winner. It came with a chance to be loved and cuddled and kissed and adored.

Hiro tried to jump out, but she was stuck deep in the seat of the stroller. She wrestled and wiggled to get herself free, to get herself to Daddy and . . .

Hiro jerked awake. Daddy was not there. Leia and the strollers were only a part of a happy memory. It was a very vivid dream, but nothing more than that. The young tuxedo cat was alone in the dark bedroom, and Daddy was far, far away.

Sadly, Hiro curled her head in under her front legs and tried to fall back into a dream of happier family times.

Artemis left the meeting of the High Council Leaders with mixed emotions. He knew he had been entrusted with monitoring the activities of two members of the royal family. It was a great honor. But normally an assignment like this was a two-way street. The cats under surveillance understand who they were and were grateful for the special agent in charge of them.

Hiro and Kimba were not like that at all. He could tell they were suspicious of his presence and resented the fact that he was watching them. It was hard to feel proud about what felt more like spying than protection. He hoped it would get better once he had explained it all to Hiro. Then she could try to win Kimba over again. Artemis was fully aware that the white cat had soured on her alien heritage because of the whole invasion scheme the year before.

The Facebook invasion plan had seemed like a good idea at the time. Artemis had been all for it and sold it to Regalus, the last special agent assigned to monitor the sisters. They had even widened the scope of the mission to include other new agents around the world. But it had ended in total failure. Regalus had been reassigned, and now all eyes were on Artemis.

He could not fail. There was too much at stake.

Hurricane sat patiently in front of the tall mirror just outside the beach showers. Her swirls of black-and-orange fur blended together in the darkness. A moment later, her contact appeared.

"Greetings. Sorry for the delay," Artemis said. "I was in a meeting."

"Is everything going forward on your end?" Hurricane asked.

"Yes," Artemis said, looking back at the sleeping form of Hiro on the split screen of his computer monitor. "I think I am making some progress there. What about your end?"

"They don't show any signs of leaving. Any time they get in the car, all of the bags have stayed in the room. It looks like any other family vacation. You should have four more days before the humans return."

From his lookout post behind her, Thunder made a sharp chirping noise. Someone was coming. Hearing the warning, Artemis gave Hurricane a quick nod and vanished. Moments later, a young couple walked by, holding hands and chatting quietly. They didn't even notice the gray-and-silver tabby or the black-and-orange tortie watching them.

Hurricane turned and wandered back into the heavy undergrowth nearby. Humans made her nervous. Some were kind to what they thought was a stray cat. Most were not. It was better to avoid them. Thunder followed close at her heels.

Working their way through the tightly woven branches of tropical bushes and vines, they finally stopped under the balcony where Kimba and Hiro's human family was staying. Typhoon and Tsunami should still be in position next to the tennis court on the other side of the building, standing guard in case the family headed for the car.

It was a pretty easy assignment. There wasn't much to do but watch and report. Of course, that also meant there was no room for mistakes. If the family headed home and the Beach Team didn't give a warning, there would be no excuse sound enough to keep them out of trouble. So they took turns on sentry duty. Thunder curled up in a pile of old leaves nearby, and Hurricane began her shift.

It should be quiet until morning, but she would take nothing for granted. Absolute vigilance was vital.

Hiro roused several hours later, but her dreams had still been upsetting. Memories got mixed up with her fears and created nightmare images of the bedroom floor piled high with clothes and suitcases. Daddy was stacking shirts into one of the bags and talking to her about how much he would miss her but that they would be back soon.

In her dream, she tried to climb over all of the mountains of clothing to get to him, but it just kept getting higher and higher. She meowed for help, but Daddy couldn't hear her. The nightmare ended as she fell asleep in the clothes, never able to reach him.

Now, awake in the empty bedroom, Hiro could sort out the real memory of Daddy talking to her while he packed the bags. He had tried to explain it all. She realized that now. But she had just been so fascinated with what seemed like the contents of every dresser drawer being piled on the bed that she hadn't paid attention. She hoped he knew that she missed him, even if she hadn't said goodbye properly.

The room was dark and very quiet, with the faint glow of the morning sun just beginning. It was time to face what came next. Daddy had left her alone, and Artemis was waiting for her to come back to the mirror. Her heart sank at the thought of it. But then that cat-like squiggle of curiosity got the better of her. There were many things she still wanted to find out from the Cat in the Mirror. There was no harm in gathering information, especially if Kimba was listening in.

Temporarily avoiding the bathroom, Hiro stalked out into the living room. In the dim light coming from Mama's office, she could see that no one else was around. After a quick visit to the laundry room for food and water, keeping her eyes open every moment for Miss Fatty Cat, Hiro went looking for Kimba. There was no way she was talking to Artemis alone.

She found her sister deep asleep on her

favorite dining room chair.

"Kimba," she whispered. "It's time."

Kimba opened one eye sleepily and then shut it again.

"Kimba," she said a bit louder, "he will know I am up and be waiting to hear from me."

With an enormous tooth-filled yawn and much dramatic stretching, claws flexed and taut, Kimba finally sat up and blinked her eyes.

"You sit outside the door, just out of view, and I'll see what else I can find out," Hiro said.

Kimba nodded slightly and then jumped down from the chair. It had taken her a few minutes to wrap her thoughts around what Hiro was talking about. She had thought she was done with all of the alien cat nonsense. Now here she was, right back in the middle of it.

At least they can't get me to use the computer, she thought. *It's all shut down, and I don't know the new password. There are no humans to spy on right now anyhow.*

She couldn't see any harm in just listening and learning.

Kimba and Hiro as kittens, enjoying a ride in
the baby strollers with their favorite toy.

Hiro still loved the stroller,
even when she was too big to fit anymore.

9

LIFE-CHANGING NEWS

Hiro marched into the bathroom and trotted straight for the mirror. Knowing that Kimba was hiding right around the corner boosted her confidence. She hopped up onto the sink and sat up tall. The image of Artemis appeared immediately, as if he had been watching and waiting.

"Greetings, Hiro," he said calmly.

"Greetings, Artemis," she answered officially.

"I hope you had a nice rest."

"Yes, thank you."

"I noticed you were no longer sleeping and was surprised you did not come in for food and water."

"Um, I went into the kitchen," she admitted, leaving out the part about talking to her sister. "It feels funny to eat and use the litter box when I know you are watching."

"Of course," Artemis nodded. "As long as you are taking care of yourself and staying healthy."

"Is that part of your job? To make sure I stay healthy?"

"Yes, I suppose it is," he admitted. "Making sure you are safe and well cared for is important. We would have to take action if we thought there might be a problem."

"Action? What kind of action?" she wondered.

"Never mind about that for now. I thought you would want to learn more about your family. That seems to be of great interest to you, as it should be."

"Yes, please," Hiro said, easily distracted. "Tell me about how we are royalty and what we are hiding from."

"Very well," he said. "Do you remember how we talked about the warrior cats who came to Earth first?"

"Yes."

"All during those millions of years, and hundreds of thousands of missions and explorations of Earth, the cats of your family, your ancestors, were in charge. Somewhere before any of those missions, your very ancient relatives were the ones who developed the technology and designed the ships that could cross the universe.

"Those ships could reach Earth and other planets like it where your large cousins could exist and breathe and eat and enjoy their adventures. None of it would have been possible without your great, great, a thousand-times-great-grandparents."

"So they were really smart," Hiro concluded.

"Very smart, and very brave, and very determined to make life better for all of their cat relatives."

Hiro nodded, but she suddenly felt very small

and unimportant. *Brave* and *smart* were the last words she would ever use to describe herself. She was forever falling off furniture or banging her head or getting thawumped by Miss Fatty Cat. Nothing she did ever made life better for anyone, except maybe for Daddy. He loved her no matter what.

"Your family is still in charge," Artemis continued.

"Right now?" she asked in shock.

"Right now. Every order I get, every mission I take, comes from members of your family."

"My cousins?"

"Yes, sometimes, but mostly your mother and father."

Hiro was too stunned to speak.

"Did you hear me, Hiro?"

She nodded and gulped, her eyes wide.

"Do you understand?"

Hiro just stared at the Cat in the Mirror, not sure how to answer.

"Your mother is the high commander. Nothing

happens on any of our ships without her permission. She runs the whole show."

That was a bit too much for Hiro to believe. It sounded more like a trick to get her to trust the alien cats. She didn't remember anything about her birth mother. She and Kimba had been only a day or two old when Daddy found them. Their eyes hadn't even opened yet. Artemis's claim that their mother was the high commander seemed pretty outlandish.

"But Regalus said my mother was here on Earth and we were separated from her. Why would someone that important be stuck on Earth?" she challenged him. *And how could she lose her babies?*

"We lost touch with an important special agent, your uncle," Artemis explained. "Using mirrors to communicate is not a perfect science, but it is the best we can do so we do not draw attention to ourselves or lose the trust of the humans. If we know where an agent is, we can use all kinds of reflective devices to make contact. Your uncle was lost and was unable to find his way back to his home base. We heard a rumor from another agent that he had been seen several blocks away from your home. But she is confined to her house, like you two, and could not get his attention.

"Your mother knew that if she could find him, he could be restored to his family. Or he could simply make reports through a car windshield if the car was always parked in the same place. She felt responsible for him. He is a member of the family, after all. She wanted to go make contact personally. No one expected you to be born so soon."

"But why did she leave us?"

Hiro tried to sound brave, but she wanted to cry. It was hard to know how to feel about the fact that coming to live with her human family had been an accident. She always knew that to some extent—that they had been separated from their cat mother—but it was worse to talk about it.

"The car we were using to stay in contact with her had been moved. When she realized that you would be born early, there was no way for her to tell us so we could bring her back.

In desperation, your mother snuck into a house under construction to look for a mirror to try to communicate and call for help. Sadly, none had been put up yet. She didn't have any way to let us know what was happening.

"We sent another special agent to help find her when we lost communications. Since she was hiding in the house, he couldn't locate her and had to return to the ship empty-handed. The High Council Leaders didn't sleep much that night, I assure you.

"After you and your sister were born, she hid you away and went to look for a car windshield or any reflective device that might work to let us know exactly where she was. Then we could retrieve all of you. But she couldn't find any active portals. While she was gone, workers came and locked up the house. She tried all night, but she couldn't get back in."

"Oh," Hiro sighed.

"So she went to find your uncle and complete her mission," he continued. "She expected to sneak back into the house the next day while the

89

workers were busy and carry you somewhere safe. When the men came back that morning, they must have found you and put you in a box. We have heard the human male tell the story of finding you that way. Before any of us at head-quarters figured out what was going on, the man already had you inside and was caring for you."

"Does she worry about us?" Hiro wondered. She didn't have any babies, but she could imagine she would worry about them if she did. She worried about Daddy, and he was a big, strong, tall human.

"At first, she was horrified. She came up with several very frantic plans to get to you. But your uncle was able to assure her that you would be well cared for."

"How could he know that?" she asked.

"The universe works in strange ways, Hiro," Artemis said.

That didn't really answer the question.

"Would you like to meet your mother?" he continued.

Hiro was too stunned to speak. *Meet her?*

"She often monitors you and keeps watch over you two. Not so much now that you are grown and she knows you are safe. But many nights, as you and Kimba slept in the bathtub nest, your mother was watching."

Their mother had been watching them? They can meet her right now? It was too much for a timid little tuxedo cat to handle.

"Kimba?" Hiro whispered. Then louder and braver, "Kimba, get in here!"

Artemis's eyes widened, and he looked over the black-and-white cat's shoulder to see Kimba slowly enter the room. His ears tipped sideways and his eyes narrowed.

"I see," he said.

Kimba leapt up on the counter next to Hiro, and the two rubbed heads. Kimba licked her sister's forehead twice to comfort her and then she faced Artemis.

"Have you been listening the whole time?" he asked.

"Yes," the white cat admitted. "I overheard you the last time. I agreed to keep watch over what you were up to so Hiro didn't get tricked into something more than she bargained for."

"Very loyal," he said. "I'm sure I would have done the same thing in your position."

The sisters stared at him, not sure what would happen next.

"Well, if you are up to date on it all, I'll repeat the question. Would you like to meet your mother?"

Kimba suspected there were parts of the story about their birth that were not exactly the truth. She had never wondered much about her cat mother. Her human mama did enough fussing and bothering for six cat parents. How would she feel if she were face-to-face with the cat who gave birth to her?

"Yes," Hiro gasped out, not waiting for her sister to ponder it further. "I'd like to meet her."

Artemis glanced over to the side at someone the sisters could not see and nodded firmly. Then he looked back at them, his azure eyes aglow.

"Greetings, My Daughters," a voice behind them said.

The sisters spun around to face a beautiful calico cat sitting right in the middle of the bathroom floor, her tail curled neatly around her front feet.

10

MOTHER

The sisters sat in stunned silence. How had she gotten here? Was this really their mother, or was it just a trick? It was creepy to have her appear in the middle of the room. Hiro thought maybe they should jump down and greet her. But Kimba didn't move, so neither did she.

"I'm sure you have hundreds of questions," the high commander said calmly. "I will immediately address the most important one. Yes, I am your real mother. I gave birth to you when I was on Earth two years ago. Everything happened just as Artemis said it did."

Hiro made a little squeaking noise, like she was going to say something but it just wouldn't come out.

"And you have been watching us ever since?" Kimba asked.

"Yes."

"How did you know where the man took us?" Kimba asked, suspicious.

"I was watching from across the street when he found you."

"Why didn't you stop him and take us with you?" Hiro finally got the courage to ask.

"Well," she explained, "first of all, the man had the black beast with him. If I had approached, that beast was certain to bark and go crazy. Any of us could have gotten hurt. Second, I wasn't sure how to interfere without risking revealing myself as more than just a stray cat. The man thought you had been abandoned and was willing to take you in and care for you. I had to admit, it was a perfect cover for you both. Much better than I could have planned."

"A cover?" Hiro asked.

"Yes," their mother said. "A perfect hiding place where no one would think to look for you."

"Artemis talked about needing to hide us too," Kimba said. "What are we hiding from? If we are really your children, shouldn't you, as high commander in charge of everyone, be able to keep us safe?"

"I am the high commander," she said, "that is true. It is a rank I was born to. But not all cats agree this is how things should be run. You have to understand, there are hundreds of ships and millions of cats in the universe. Some are involved in operations around Earth. Others are light-years away in other galaxies. When we send a message to them, it takes years to arrive. It is very hard to govern the whole thing and not make some cats feel left out. There are rebel groups who would like to change how things are run."

"But why would they worry about us?" Kimba asked.

"Do you understand what it means to *inherit* something?" she asked.

Kimba shook her head. Hiro just stared and blinked, trying hard to follow everything that was being said. She was so grateful Kimba was there.

"You inherit something when it is passed down to you from your parents or your family. It might be the color and type of your fur. It could also be more tangible things. Humans pass on money and houses and valuable art or jewelry to their children. That is part of their inheritance as a member of the family. You, My Daughters, have inherited many things from your father and me."

"Like the color of our fur?" Kimba said.

"And the authority to one day be high commander and be in charge of every cat in the universe. The humans would call you each a princess."

Hiro thought about the movies she had watched with Mindy and Leia. There were often cartoon princesses who wore fancy dresses and had long flowing hair. She couldn't quite see how that would apply to a cat.

"In human history, royal families have run everything. They were in charge of the government and the armies and every last thing that happened in their kingdom. Where you live, in this country, there is no royal family. There are many people in charge. America fought for this democracy and freedom. Humans here vote and elect their leaders.

"Some cats have watched this system develop over the last few hundred years we have monitored Earth. To them, it seems like a better way to govern things. They want our system of power to be like that too. No more royal family in charge, only cats elected by popular vote to be high commander and on the High Council."

"Would that be such a bad thing?" Kimba asked.

"It is just not practical for us. Elections and many different individuals vying for power can be a very dangerous process. Human history has proven this to be true as well. It can lead to wars and violent battles for power. Conflicts like that have not ever been a part of cat life in the universe. We live in harmony and care for each other's needs.

"Also, cats from one ship to another have very little contact. How in the world would they all decide on who should be high commander and who should be on the Council? It just does not make sense. It does not need to happen. But there are still groups that are determined to rise to power. It is not really about being fair or wanting to have justice and opportunities for all cats. It is about putting themselves in power and removing our family from our rightful position, a position we have held for longer than anyone can remember."

Kimba thought about the TV shows she had watched with Mama. Kings had to fight to protect their kingdoms. There always seemed to be someone who wanted to take it over and be the new king. She had never thought about cats having the same problems. In her house, the humans took care of all of their needs. She was quite happy to let Mama and Daddy be in charge.

"Is there a war going on?" Kimba asked.

Hiro stared at her with wide eyes. She had seen those movies too.

"It has not come to that yet," their mother said. "We really don't have any need of weapons on our ships. We have toured the universe peacefully for millions of years. War, like your humans seem to be always in the middle of, is just not a part of our heritage. But we have been watching and interacting with humans so much that the idea has rubbed off on some of our more disgruntled members. I have begun to think that maybe it is time to get off these ships and settle down on a planet where all cats can live together."

"Is that why you want to take over? Why you wanted Kimba to help you get into Mama's Facebook page and organize an invasion?" Hiro sputtered.

But she never expected what came next. Her mother lifted her chin resolutely.

"There was never going to be any invasion."

Kimba gasped and sat frozen. Hiro's eyes narrowed. She and Kimba had talked about the events of those weeks of their kitten lives many times. Hiro may not have been a part of all of it, but she was very clear on what Kimba had been asked to do. Kimba was supposed to help with a cat invasion of Earth. Not following through with her mission had been a huge failure to the other agent cats.

"That doesn't make any sense," Hiro said. "Kimba had a mission to help set up an invasion."

"Yes," the high commander said without flinching, "that is what her mission was. She was directed to follow very specific steps to help support her cat family. She did not complete this mission."

"She let everyone down, and the invasion failed," Hiro said bluntly.

Kimba flicked her tail in agitation and glared at her sister, but she didn't say anything.

"Well, she did let everyone down, and the mission failed, but there was never any real invasion plan," their mother admitted.

She waited for this to sink in. Kimba's ears flushed pink, but she didn't know what to say. Hiro just twitched her whiskers, trying to understand. It didn't make sense. Their mother sighed.

"It was a test," she said flatly.

"A test?" Kimba repeated in disbelief.

"Yes," she said. "We would never have really trusted such a huge mission to a new and young recruit."

"Did Regalus know it was only a test?" Hiro gasped.

"No. If he had, he might have let on somehow or not been so urgent about getting Kimba's cooperation. He was just as much a part of the test as you and Kimba."

"Me?"

"Of course. And there were many more new agents involved all over the world. The time will come when we are ready to send a large group from the ship to Earth. We need to know exactly how and when this can be done most effectively. Your refusal to allow any harm to come to the humans gave us vital information about how cats bond with their caregivers.

"We were quite impressed that you were willing to risk so much to protect your human family. In a way, you did help to delay our plans to occupy

Earth. Your devotion to the people you live with gave us hope that the humans are worth continued study. It was surprising how few Earth cats were willing to cooperate. Clearly, there is still much we need to learn. We have especially been watching you, Hiro, and the human male. You two have a very rare and interesting relationship. We have enjoyed studying it over the last months."

"You have still been studying it?"

"Yes. As you know, we can always see you, even if you can't see us."

Hiro's stomach felt queasy and odd. Part of her never wanted to come into the bathroom again. The other part ached with a longing for Daddy's comfort.

"That's enough for now," Artemis said from the mirror behind them.

The sisters turned to face him.

"The risk seems slight, since the humans are on an extended vacation, but we do not like having the high commander away from the ship and vulnerable for too long."

"We can talk more later," their mother said quietly. "Maybe next time you can come visit me."

"Come visit you?" Kimba asked. "Like to your ship, out in space?"

"Yes," she said matter-of-factly. "We have been fully prepared to pull you out of this home if you ever seemed in danger. It is a simple process, if you know exactly where the individual is. As long as we know where you are, we can pull you up to the ship in a moment. That has always been the plan. If you were ever in danger, or if the humans were unkind to you, we could retrieve you and bring you home."

"Let's just take one step at a time," Artemis said uneasily. "Kimba and Hiro already have quite a lot to think about. You two should come back to the mirror later today after the human grandmother has come and gone again. We can talk more then."

"Will you come back too?" Hiro turned and asked their mother.

"Possibly. Artemis is devoted to your care and keeping me informed about how you are doing. But if I am needed, I will come."

She looked up at Artemis in the mirror, gave a quick nod, there was a bright light in the bathrooom, and then she vanished. Kimba and Hiro stared at the empty spot where she had been and blinked in disbelief. Did the Cats in the Mirror have the power to make one of them vanish just as quickly?

Hiro looked back at the mirror to ask Artemis just that, but he was already gone as well. The bathroom was quiet and so still that she could hear Kimba's rapid breathing. The white cat jumped down from the counter and stalked intently out of the bathroom and around the corner out of sight. Hiro raced to follow her.

Outside the door, the two just sat and thought about everything they had learned. Then Kimba said something that made Hiro's blood run cold.

"If Artemis could pluck us right out of our house any time he wanted, could the other cats, the ones who don't like our family, do the same thing? If they know where we are, can they just take us away?"

And was there anything the Cats in the Mirror could do to save them?

11

BIG DECISION

The sisters spent the next hour worrying, not moving from the spot outside the bathroom door. They didn't say much of anything out loud, but having each other close while pondering what they had learned was a comfort.

They thought long and hard about all of the amazing new information their mother had shared with them. Their mother? Even that was fascinating all by itself. She was truly regal and sophisticated and every bit of what a high commander should be. Hiro found it hard to believe she was related to such a magnificent cat. Kimba, on the other hand, thought it was completely logical.

Hiro was intrigued by the three colors in her mother's fur: white and black and brown. Hiro knew that combination didn't happen very often, just like how Kimba's eyes were two different colors. It was rare and special. Hiro thought she should look more closely at her own fur to see if she could find any splotches of brown she might have inherited from her beautiful mother.

But right now, the realization that the Cats in the Mirror had the power to somehow transfer them to the ship at any moment totally occupied their thoughts. If the agents could do it, that must mean the rebels could do it too.

As shocking as it was, Kimba's fear had a sound basis. It was creepy to think that strange cats, especially those who don't like your family and might want to cause you harm, could pull you away from everything you love, maybe never to come back again.

Just the thought of being taken away from

Daddy was more than Hiro could bear. Her back had started twitching and jumping, and her tail lashed. She hunkered down next to her sister, hoping it would go away. But her tail just curled up toward her like a possessed snake and swished from side to side. As a kitten, a twitchy back and flicky tail would have led to an obsessive game of chase-the-tail. She had a bit more self-control now. But only just a little bit, so she hoped it would calm down soon.

Kimba noticed the jumping and thrashing and hoped it would settle down soon too. There was no time for distractions like that. She needed Hiro's full attention.

"First of all, we need to find out if I am right. We need to know if the angry cats can get to us."

Hiro nodded in agreement.

"But before we talk to Artemis and our mother again, we need to decide if we will take her up on her invitation."

"What invitation?" Hiro asked, the tics on her back convulsing like an earthquake tremor. She gave the most misbehaving parts a quick lick, trying to relax the muscles a bit. Her tail jerked, but she refused to start the chase.

"She asked us to come visit her on the ship. Don't you remember?"

Hiro had forgotten about that part.

"We could see what the inside of the ship looks like," Kimba said. "We could see what the room where Artemis sits looks like and how all the computers work. We might even be able to look into this bathroom from out in space!"

Kimba was fascinated by the idea of a bit of adventure. Deep in her heart, there was still a curious kitten who just had to know what was on the other side of the door.

Hiro was not so sure.

"What if we can't get back?" she asked her daring sister. "What if we get stuck? Or what if our mother wants us to stay and won't send us back? What if it is all just a trick?"

Kimba didn't have any answers. She would miss her human family. But as long as she knew they were safe, she didn't worry about getting stuck. *Would it be so bad to live on a spaceship? There would be so much to explore!*

"I don't want to live without Daddy," Hiro said quietly.

Kimba knew it. Hiro would never agree to stay where she couldn't see Daddy every day. Being separated during this vacation was already taking its toll on her nerves. Just watching her sister's back contort, she knew there was no chance of her agreeing to go away forever.

"We can talk about it more later," Kimba assured her. "You look like you could use a nap."

Hiro nodded and slunk under the bed. Every conversation with the Cats in the Mirror left her totally exhausted. She just wanted to sleep. But first she needed to force her tail to behave.

As Kimba wandered from the room, she could hear telltale thunking and thrashing sounds from under the bed. Hiro would chase her tail until she collapsed from exhaustion. Some things never changed.

And some things did. Kimba realized that if she went up to visit the ship, her life in this small Earthbound house would never be the same.

Kimba, sleeping cuddled up with Mickey Mouse
and some of Mama's stuffed animal collection.

12

IS IT SAFE?

Kimba slept restlessly in her special bed up high on Mama's bookshelf. Every one of the stuffed animals in the collection was all tidy and in place. This was Kimba's favorite spot in the whole house. But today she was reminded of a time nearly a year ago when she had spent another sleepless night deciding whether or not to cooperate with the alien cats. Special Agent Regalus had given her a mission to help plan a cat invasion of Earth. Fears for the safety of her human family had made her refuse to complete that mission.

But this time it didn't sound like the family was in danger at all. This risk was about her own safety and whether or not she should make a trip to outer space to learn more about her cat family. Curiosity niggled at her and whispered into her sleepy brain that there would be new nooks and crannies to explore and new adventures to be had.

Another part of her remembered how excited she had been to escape from the confines of this house to explore outside. That much-anticipated adventure had been a terrifying disaster. Outdoors had been nothing like she had dreamed. What if the spaceship was the same?

In her favorite special spot under Mama and Daddy's bed, Hiro fought with sleep too. Her tail was behaving itself now, but her thoughts raced. She was curious to see the inside of the ship and to learn more about her family. That part she couldn't deny. But the idea of being transferred up to the ship was alarming.

How did it work? Did it hurt? It was not even an option unless she was positive beyond a shadow of a doubt that she could get back to Daddy. He may have left her alone for a few days, but they would never be apart forever. Not if she could help it.

Hiro heard a soft thunk in the other room. Moments later, footsteps swished through the living room carpet. Peeking out from under the bed, she saw her sister's four white feet coming across the bedroom toward her. Kimba peered under the bed.

"Are you still awake?" she whispered.

"Yes," Hiro said. "You can't sleep either?"

"No, so we may as well talk it out."

Kimba slipped under the bed and hunkered down next to her sister. The light coming through the big bedroom window was beginning to fade. Grandma would be there soon for her daily visit. After that, they were supposed to go back to the mirror. Of course, they were supposed to be well rested by then too.

"What if it's a trick?" Hiro asked.

"A trick to get us up on the ship?"

"Yes. Like all of that stuff with the invasion was just a trick to test your loyalty."

"But if they wanted to pull us up to the ship, couldn't they just do it, with or without our permission?"

Hiro raised her head, looking up toward the sky. *What a terrifying thought!*

"Do the angry cats have the power to do the same thing if they want to?" Kimba continued. "Artemis said we are hiding from them. If we go to the ship, does that make us easier to find?"

They fell silent, neither of them having the answers they needed.

"Mother said they have been watching us since we were born," Kimba said. "Regalus, and now Artemis, and who knows how many others, have been keeping track of us to ensure our safety. So why would she want us to do something dangerous? Would Artemis even allow it if we could get hurt?"

"You want to go, don't you," Hiro said quietly.

Kimba didn't answer, but her ears and nose flushed a bright pink in the dim light under the bed.

"If you want to go," Hiro said timidly, "and

116

you think it is safe, and we can get back home, I will go."

"We know what questions to ask to be sure it is safe," Kimba said. "We will just have to watch how Artemis answers them. Remember how edgy Regalus would get sometimes? If we feel like they are lying to us, we won't go."

"Agreed."

Hiro's eyes started to droop. Having that settled, she knew it was way past nap time. Just like their big cat cousins, little cats need many hours of sleep each day. The sisters were exhausted.

"We can catch a bit of rest before Grandma comes," Kimba said.

Hiro nodded in agreement. Her sister adjusted her body so the two were curled up against each other, like they used to sleep every night when they were just tiny kittens in their bathtub nursery. Basking in the comforting warmth and closeness of her sister, Hiro quickly fell into a deep sleep.

Buddy hunkered in the bushes near the front door. It was nearly time for Grandma to come by and pour some food into the bowl on the front porch for him. Years ago, he would not have felt so dependent on a human to provide his meals. Now, as he grew older, hunting was not as thrilling or exciting as it used to be. It was easier to just bide his time and eat the stale crunchy bits that passed as food. It provided the necessary nutriments.

Once the kittens were a bit older, Buddy knew he would be free of his responsibility to guard their house so diligently. Maybe he would even be able to end his Earth mission altogether. He had lucked upon a good human family years ago when they found him in the woods. They let him come and go as he pleased, and they even welcomed him back with open arms after he was gone for over a year.

After all of his trips to Earth over so many years, this one had been special to him. Sitting alone in the bushes, Buddy could remember Leia as a toddler, trying to carry him across the yard. She wasn't much bigger than he was. Getting him under the front legs as best as she could, she had mostly dragged him along. His bottom had bumped against the ground, and she nearly stepped on his tail several times, but he didn't mind. Many a happy winter night had been spent curled up on her bed.

They had shown him what it meant to be a part of a human family. For many years, he had actually enjoyed being "owned" and not having much else to do but monitor and report. He knew he didn't have anything to complain about, but he was just weary of the whole thing. When this mission was over, he would not return to Earth again. He was sure High Commander Felicity would understand.

Felicity could be proud of her daughters. Kimba and Hiro had proven to be fiercely loyal to their human family, the only parents they knew. Now it was her job to shift that devotion to where it really belonged. Cats should be faithful and honorable to cats, to their rightful heritage. As much as he had enjoyed the company of these humans during his

Earth-life, he was ready to go home.

Once Grandma had come and gone and night had fallen, Buddy could jump on the hood of Mindy's car and check in with his brother to see how it was going with the cats inside the house. He had given up hope that the sisters would ever be in contact with the Cats in the Mirror again. But now that they were willing to talk, he hoped Artemis could win Kimba and Hiro over quickly.

After a nice nap, Artemis checked back in with the agent on watch. The sisters had not returned to the bathroom mirror, and the grandmother had not stopped by yet. Of course, the agent would have awoken him immediately if either of those events had taken place.

Resuming his position at the computer console, Artemis split the screen view so he could contact the high commander in her quarters.

High Commander Felicity was awake and actively considering what her next steps should be. Even stretched out on her favorite fluffy pillow, she could not find comfort. The High Council Leaders had agreed to allow her a brief visit with her daughters. She was grateful they had let her go down to the surface of Earth again. The last time had been such a disaster, she was not confident they would let her repeat the process.

Protecting her safety was the only time the High Council had control over her actions. The transfer to visit her daughters in their human home was important, and the Leaders had understood that. It was logical that seeing her in the flesh would help make Kimba and Hiro feel more attached to her and to their heritage. She needed them to understand exactly what their destiny was and why their lives were so important.

It was possible Kimba and Hiro could spend their whole Earth-lives with this human family. As the youngest of her children, they had many siblings in line before them. But their presence could still be required if the rebellion got out of hand. It could also put their safety in jeopardy.

If only I could ship those obnoxious, rebellious,

troublemaking cats to Earth and dump them in the wilderness somewhere, she thought. That would teach them to question her authority.

Her ancestors had never had to deal with such upstart and ambitious creatures. *The humans are definitely a bad influence.*

Her tail thrashed, and her whiskers stood out straight in frustration. The flashing red light on her computer forced her to regain her composure. She clicked on her screen and faced Artemis.

"Greetings. Did you rest well, High Commander?" he asked politely.

"Yes, thank you, just fine, Special Agent Artemis."

"Before I communicate with Kimba and Hiro again, it would be wise for us to discuss something as drastic as bringing them aboard the ship."

"You disagree with this strategy?"

"It just seems rather dangerous. My primary responsibility is to be sure the children are safe."

"And I appreciate that, Artemis. Yes, any transfer from Earth to the ship comes with some risk," she agreed, "but I'm not sure they really

122

believe us about where they come from and who they are. They don't understand it all in their hearts. Having me appear in the bathroom was an effective stunt. I think it helped. But if they could see the ship with their own eyes, then it would be easier to gain their loyalty."

"But why the rush? We have time."

"To gain their loyalty and trust, yes. To remove them from the house for an extended period without alarming the humans, there is no time like the present. We still have a few days before the family should return. Just the absence of the humans is making my daughters more willing to talk with us again. We should not waste this opportunity."

"If they are not willing to make the transfer?"

Artemis hesitated to say out loud what he knew Felicity was already aware of.

"I know. If they resist at all it can . . . well, it can all go very wrong."

"Even if one of them becomes afraid and panics. Why should we take a chance with your daughters?"

"I'm not sure we should. But we at least need to consider it and see if they are willing to try. That is all," she said abruptly and closed the communication window with a swift tap.

The high commander should not have to argue with an agent. She would make the decision, and everyone would obey.

But she knew Artemis was right. There was always a risk of losing a cat who panicked during the transfer. She had been on hand to see complications with more than one Earth delivery. It wasn't a perfect science, but they had been using it for millions of years to transport cat cousins of every shape and size to Earth and other planets. It worked just fine, most of the time.

She glanced over at her mate, Griffin, as he slept stretched out on his pillow. His long, thick coat of black-and-white fur made him look twice his size and very imposing when it came to dealing with the rebels. Felicity was proud she had chosen her partner well. It was too bad her daughters on Earth had not inherited his wonderful fur. She returned to her pillow next to him in the hopes of getting a bit of sleep.

There was nothing to do now but wait until her daughters came back to the mirror. She understood Artemis's hesitation about transferring the girls to the ship. But what if there came a time in all of this conflict when the sisters really were in danger? If the rebels found them and wanted to get at them, Felicity would have to act quickly. It would be safer if they already knew what to expect and could cooperate in an emergency. Transferring an unwilling or scared cat was out of the question.

This is just part of their training, she concluded.

Kimba and Hiro needed to know their options and how to escape from a threat the humans couldn't begin to imagine or protect them from. Her moles, hidden deep in the rebel group, would alert her of any impending danger for her sons and daughters, wherever they may be. Hopefully, she would be able to help them all escape if the time came.

Felicity was not worried about Kimba. She would make the shift just fine. She might even want to stay. Hiro, on the other hand, would need to be handled carefully. Above all, she must not panic.

That would be disastrous.

Buddy and little Leia.

13

TIME TO GO

Hiro stirred from her nap and realized the room was pitch dark. There was a dripping noise from the bathroom as droplets of water from the tub faucet splashed down into the puddle of water below and echoed off the white walls and tile floor.

Plink. Plink. Plink.

Did Grandma come and run water in the tub? she wondered. *Did we sleep through it all?*

Kimba stirred next to her. Her sister's ears pricked up as she caught the dripping sound too.

"Grandma was already here," Kimba concluded.

Hiro peeked out from under the bed. The bathroom was dark, but her eyes adjusted quickly. Her pupils opened wide to let any bit of light reflect on the back of her eyes to help her see.

Not ready to be observed by the Cats in the Mirror just yet, the sisters slunk out of the bedroom and into the kitchen to their special cat room. The lamp from Mama's office, set to go on automatically in the evening, gave them just enough light to take care of the business of eating and drinking and visiting the litter box. Hiro hated sharing a drinking bowl, but it smelled fresh. Miss Fatty Cat and Slinky must have slept through Grandma's visit too and not drunk from it yet.

Her belly full of food and water, Hiro stepped out into the kitchen.

"Be alert!" Kimba hissed behind her.

Thawump.

Too late. All fifteen pounds of Miss Fatty Cat landed on Hiro's back. The black cat lay there for a bit, as if savoring the moment, and then she lazily got up and faced Kimba. The white cat laid her ears back and hissed.

"Mess with my sister, mess with me!" she threatened.

"Oh, get over it," Miss Fatty Cat said and waddled away into the dining room.

Hiro staggered to her feet and attempted to lick her rumpled fur back into place. A messy coat was easier to fix than hurt dignity. Kimba licked her sister's head several times and rubbed against her face.

"Okay now?" she asked.

"Yeah. I should know better. She can hear the food crunching from anywhere in the house and comes right for me. Maybe we can get Artemis to transfer that stupid fat cat up to the ship and keep her there."

"That's a thought," Kimba said, perking up her ears.

Who knows what trouble Miss Fatty Cat might get into if she started working with the Cats in the Mirror? Hiro thought. *What if she ever got mixed up with the angry rebel alien cats?* She'd turn the sisters over in a heartbeat. Hiro was sure of it.

She knew Artemis must be watching for them by now. It seemed rude to keep him waiting since it could have been hours already since Grandma left. Knowing the events of her life were being monitored made Hiro's spine tingle. It would be nice to think she had some privacy.

Without a word, the sisters trotted back into the bedroom and on through to the bathroom. Kimba was beginning to flush with excitement.

Will they transfer us to the ship right now? Can we ask questions first? she wondered.

Kimba and Hiro jumped deftly onto the counter in front of the big mirror and waited. When nothing happened, Hiro let out a little chirp to get the attention of whoever was on watch. The mirror lit up a bit, got fuzzy, and then Artemis slowly came into focus.

"Greetings, Kimba and Hiro," he said. "I trust that you are well rested and ready. Your mother would like you to visit the ship and see more about where you come from. You need to under-stand who you are if you are ever going to be a part of this life."

The high commander had been right. Once she made the decision to bring her daughters to the ship and gave the order to have it carried out, all discussion ceased. Artemis obeyed her without comment.

He's just going to get right to it, Hiro thought with a terrified gulp.

"We have some concerns first," Kimba spoke up.

"Go ahead."

"First, we want you to promise that we will be returned right here to this room before our human family gets back. You have been studying us. You know Hiro needs to be with Daddy."

Hiro nodded, her eyes wide.

"I promise you will be returned to your Earth home," he said confidently. "You are safe there for now, and the High Council has no intention of bringing you permanently to the ship for many years."

Kimba's ears twitched at the last part of his promise.

"So they do intend to bring us there someday," she said.

"Well, of course. A cat only spends a handful of years alive on Earth. Some make it to twenty years old, but that is still only a portion of your life. A cat life goes on for hundreds of years."

Hiro and Kimba stared at each other and then back at Artemis.

"How does that work, exactly?" Hiro asked. "Daddy would worry about me if I just vanished one day."

"Of course he would, and so would all the other cat lovers on Earth if their pets vanished. Any time we make a transfer from Earth to the ship, we are really just moving your essence. The humans call it things like a soul or spirit. Your body is simply how you think about yourself, so it can come with you or stay behind. Once your Earth-body is worn out, or if some kind of sickness or accident happens, then we pull that essence back to the ship and leave the earthly shell behind.

Here, you start fresh again."

"Like heaven?" Hiro whispered.

"No, not at all. That's something some humans believe happens after they die. Any cat on Earth is just undercover, in a sense. It is a temporary arrangement. Some agents love it on Earth and choose to go back over and over again during their lifetime. Once is enough for some. Some never want to go.

"The ones who are born on Earth, like you two, have a choice to make. Sadly, most of them don't know they have anywhere else to go. They have never been in contact with us, and we don't have any way to know what is happening in their lives. Those cats don't get a choice to live out their full centuries of life. They think Earth-life is all there is. When you understand who you really are and what your options are, you can decide to stay on the ship or go back to Earth in cat form."

That was all a bit much for Hiro. Sitting in the dark bathroom with Daddy hundreds of miles away and talking about death frayed her nerves. She felt dizzy, and she hunkered down next to her sister. Kimba just stood taller.

"So you promise we can come back," she said, trying not to get caught up in the rest of what Artemis had said.

"Absolutely."

"Okay, then we also need to know if this is safe. It seems a little crazy to just disappear in one place and show up miles away out in space."

"Thousands of miles, actually," Artemis corrected.

That didn't help Hiro at all. Her heart felt like it would pound out of her chest. Kimba pursed her whiskers.

"Fine, *thousands* of miles away."

"We have been making these transfers daily for millions of years. Agents come and go. Adventure seekers go back and forth for a few days. It is all very routine."

"Does anything ever go wrong?"

Artemis did a slight look away from the sisters and off at someone else in the room with him.

There it was. That was the sign. Kimba knew

that meant he was lying or keeping something from them. Regalus had always made that same twitchy move when he was being tricky.

"So it does! It does go wrong!" she accused him.

Before he had time to answer, the image in the mirror flickered and shifted so that it was now a split screen image, like when Daddy watched two football games at the same time on the big TV in the living room. Artemis was on one side of the mirror, and their mother appeared on the other side.

"Greetings, My Daughters," Felicity said.

Hiro sat up straight and tried to look dignified. Kimba twitched her ears, not sure what to expect.

"Do not be wary of Special Agent Artemis," she continued. "He has only one mission, and that is to ensure your care and safety. He is not trying to trick you into doing something dangerous. But there are some cautions you should be aware of."

"So we need to be cautious?" Hiro whispered. "Is it dangerous?"

"This transfer is no more dangerous than driving in a human car or flying in an airplane.

Sometimes those machines can cause harm to the humans using them, but there is usually some lack of care or unsafe behavior from one of the humans that leads to an accident. You two are very high-profile guests. Only the best special agents and most skilled operators will be involved."

Hiro crouched back down, but Kimba stood tall and tried to appear confident. Felicity gazed down at Hiro, her eyes filled with loving concern.

"The only danger there can be today is if one of you overreacts or gets scared and fights the transfer."

Kimba looked from her mother to her sister, still hunkered down next to her. Hiro's eyes were full of fear.

"Maybe Hiro shouldn't try to do this just yet," Artemis suggested, more to the high commander than to the sisters. "I am sensing great amounts of fear and anxiety from her. It would not be safe."

"What do you think, Hiro?" her mother asked.

Kimba looked from her mother to her sister again. She would rather have Hiro with her, setting out into outer space together, but not if there were any danger to her. She licked the top of Hiro's head a few times to help calm her nerves.

Hiro took a deep breath. She wasn't so sure she should try it yet either. Maybe if Kimba went first. Her sister had always been braver and more excited to explore and try new adventures.

"Will we end up near to where you are now?" Hiro asked her mother timidly.

"Yes, the transfer area is quite near to us," she assured her.

"If Kimba goes first, and I can see her in the mirror looking back at me and know that it is all right, then I will be ready to do it myself. Is that okay, Kimba?"

Her ears flushed pink, but Kimba nodded her agreement. As scared as she was to be shot through space somehow, who knew when this chance would come again? She was ready.

"Special Agent Artemis," Felicity said, "please make preparations to transfer Kimba on board."

The sisters watched as Artemis tapped on a keyboard below him and whispered directions to

137

another cat they could not see, standing nearby. Then he looked back at the sisters, his blue eyes aglow in the dark room.

"Kimba, please go sit in the middle of the bathroom, where the high commander was yesterday. It helps if there is nothing around you to interfere or get caught up in the collection."

Kimba jumped down quickly, her heart racing, and sat up tall in the same spot her mother had been only hours before. Somehow, in that moment, she felt pride in that heritage and destiny that Regalus had rattled on and on about. She was not just a house cat who would live a few years with a human family. Her real life and destiny lay in the stars.

"Are you ready, Kimba?" Artemis asked.

"Yes, I am ready."

"It is very important that you just relax and let go. Imagine it to be like when the human woman picks you up. Don't fight, just allow yourself to be lifted. You will feel a tingling sensation. Then everything will be very bright for a second. Just close your eyes and count slowly to ten. Before you reach ten, you will be here."

Kimba nodded her understanding. She looked up at Hiro, still crouched on the counter.

"It will be okay, Hiro. You'll see."

Hiro blinked slowly back at her sister. She had never really thought about what she would do if something happened to Kimba. She just expected they would always be together. Hiro gripped the corner of the countertop with her claws and held her breath.

"Ready?" Artemis asked.

"Yes."

"Okay," he said, keeping his voice calm and level, "then on five, four, three, two, one . . . now."

There was a flash of light. Then Kimba was gone.

Hiro gasped as the reality of her sister vanishing in front of her eyes sunk in. She spun around to face the Cats in the Mirror, but both her mother and Artemis were intently focused on something across the room.

Count to ten, Hiro thought. *One, two, three, four, five, six, seven . . .*

She saw her mother let out a big sigh, and Artemis began to nod calmly. Felicity looked back at Hiro and lifted her ears high.

"She is here, Hiro, and everything is fine."

"Can I see Kimba, please?" Hiro said. "I just need to see her."

"Of course. Give her a moment."

Hiro waited expectantly, her back twitching and jumping, while Artemis was busy with his keypad and their mother watched across the room as her daughter approached. Then Felicity moved aside and Kimba appeared in her place.

Kimba is a Cat in the Mirror!

"Greetings, Hiro," Kimba teased, her eyes wide with excitement.

"Amazing," Hiro said. "You are in outer space!"

"I know!" Kimba said. Her nose and ears were almost red with the thrill of it. "The transfer is like nothing at all, Hiro. Don't be scared. It just feels like Mama is scratching your back, there's a bright light, then you are here before you know it. It's amazing! You have to come see it, or you'll never believe me!"

"And they promised we can come back."

"You heard Artemis. They want us hidden on Earth for a long time to come. We can go back before the family comes home."

"Okay." Hiro looked over to Artemis. "Let's do it quickly, before I change my mind."

She jumped down and sat in the assigned spot on the bathroom floor.

"Remember," Artemis said, "just relax and let yourself be lifted. Count to ten slowly, and don't panic or try to move. Do you understand?"

"I do," Hiro said, her heart racing and every muscle in her body taut. Her back twitched again.

Relax, she thought, *he said I have to relax.*

She tried to think of something to calm herself down. She closed her eyes and imagined lying curled up in that warm spot right next to Daddy on the bed. He would be home soon. Then he would wrap his arm around her and she would purr and sleep peacefully for the first time in days.

Suddenly, she felt a tingling along her spine,

like Mama scritchy-scratching her back. Even with her eyes shut, she could see the bright light. Fighting the urge to move and forcing a desperate meow back down her throat, she counted slowly.

One, two, three, four, five, six, seven, eight, nine . . .

THE SHIP

J ust when she was about to panic, the light and tingling stopped and everything was calm. A deep voice in front of her greeted the little black-and-white cat.

"Welcome, Hiro."

She opened her eyes to see a cat who looked like Buddy must have looked when he was young and not so beaten up. He had an amazing mane of long black fur, but his chest and a stripe up his nose were white, just like hers.

"I am Commander Griffin. We are grateful you

have agreed to visit us."

Hiro blinked and felt a little woozy, but she was quickly distracted by the sights and sounds around her. She was really there, on the spaceship!

The room was dimly lit. It took her a moment to focus, especially as her eyes recovered from the blinding light of the transfer. Looking around, Hiro realized she was sitting on a raised platform in the middle of a huge high-ceilinged room. You could fit a hundred of her Earth houses inside of it and have room left over.

This is headquarters!

All around the edges and scattered here and there were cats of all colors and sizes. Most were sitting at large desk-type areas with computer monitors in front of them. Hiro was startled to find them all staring directly at her.

"Come with me, Hiro," Griffin said. "Your sister and your mother are waiting for you."

Hiro climbed slowly down the steps in front of her and joined him on the main floor. As they walked along, every eye followed them. Blinking red lights flashed on desktops here and there, but no one moved to answer them.

Somewhere far away, Hiro could hear the hum of what must be the engine. Her sensitive feet could feel the vibrations of it through the dark tile floor.

"Is this the whole ship?" she whispered.

Griffin chuckled to himself and shook his head.

"Goodness, no. This is just one of the control rooms. We try to limit the cats on a ship to around ten million at a time, but sometimes there are more. That's when we offer special deals and incentives to transfer down to Earth for fifteen or twenty years."

Trying to imagine ten million cats so close to her boggled Hiro's mind. It was too big a number to imagine. She just knew it meant more than she could count if she spent all day trying, and that was impressive.

"As you may suspect, each of these special agents is monitoring a mirror portal somewhere on Earth. Some are in contact with agents on a specific mission. Some are monitoring situations we simply find interesting to study, like the bathrooms in human schools and businesses. The nonsense that goes on in there is fascinating. A very select and honored few are keeping tabs on special cats like you and your sister. Artemis is one of those special agents."

Griffin and Hiro stopped next to a desk where Artemis was sitting. Hiro recognized him immediately.

"Welcome, Hiro," he said formally.

"Thank you, Special Agent Artemis," she said, trying to appear proper and formal too.

His whiskers twitched, and his ears perked up. Hiro took this as a sign of approval. Artemis looked over at Griffin and bowed his head slightly.

"Commander, once we saw that the transfer was successful, the high commander took Kimba to the dining hall to prepare a snack. The transfer process tends to leave one hungry, so she wanted to address that need first. They are waiting for you there."

Hiro's stomach growled in response, and she realized he was right. She was suddenly starving.

"Thank you, Artemis. We will join them there."

Griffin began to move again, and Hiro quickly followed him. They passed through the control room and into a long, quiet hallway. There wasn't much to look at there, so Hiro just trotted quickly to keep up.

"The high commander is my mother, right?" Hiro asked shyly, not sure if it was impolite to ask questions.

"Yes," Griffin answered without seeming put out at all.

"And you are the commander?"

"Yes."

"I see," Hiro said, but it really had not answered the question she wanted to ask.

Griffin seemed to sense what she was getting at.

"Each ship is run by a High Council. Most have thirty Leaders, representing different sections of the ship. They help keep things running smoothly and alert the Council of any problems that need addressing. High Council Leaders are selected by the commanders."

"So you and my mother pick who is on the Council?"

"Yes."

"And Mother is high commander because that is passed down from her parents before her who were high commanders too."

"Exactly. Very good, Hiro."

"Is that how you got to be a commander? Were your parents commanders before you?"

"No." He shook his head and pursed his whiskers. "But my father was selected for the High Council once. That is how I met your mother."

Hiro wanted to ask more, but it might be a sensitive subject. Maybe he had battled someone for the job, like the kings and queens in the movies on TV. Maybe he had killed someone!

Griffin stopped walking and sat down to face the little tuxedo cat next to him. Hiro felt he was about to say something important, so she sat down expectantly.

"Hiro, I am commander because your mother selected me."

"Okay," Hiro said, feeling there was more to

it than that. He was looking at her very intently.

"The high commander selects another cat to be the second in command."

"That sounds like a great honor," she added.

"It is," he agreed. "The commander is also her mate, what humans call a *husband*. Do you understand?"

Griffin stared at her so directly that she hated to admit she thought she was missing something. This huge black-and-white cat was sort of married to her mother. It took Hiro a second to reach the next logical step. Her eyes narrowed, and her tail began to twitch. Her ears tipped and spun as she thought it through and made sure she really did understand. She stared back into Griffin's yellow-green eyes. He nodded slowly and blinked at her calmly. Hiro had to say it out loud to be sure it was true.

"That means that if the high commander is my mother, and you are her mate, then you must be . . . you must be . . . my father."

"Exactly. Good girl," he said, immediately

standing back up and continuing down the hall-way.

Hiro followed him in stunned silence. Never for a moment had she thought about having a cat father. Daddy was all she had ever needed. She couldn't quite sort out how she felt about knowing this huge beast of a cat was her father. She felt very small trotting along next to him.

While she was still considering this new information, they arrived at the dining hall. It was not as large as the computer room and much brighter, with white walls and tile floors. The ceilings were lower, and it didn't echo quite so much. A smell, like when Daddy opened a bag of cat food, wafted past her. It was the same odor, but somehow brighter and fresher.

Just like the computer room, the dining area was full of a wide variety of cats. Mats and pillows were laid out in sections around the room, and small groups of cats lounged there, sharing plates of food. Hiro didn't recognize what they were eating, but it looked like what Leia and Mindy called sushi. The girls got very excited about it as a special treat. It smelled amazing, but they would never let the cats have any.

Griffin changed directions, and Hiro saw they were now aiming for a raised section in the middle of the room. It was covered by a thick, white, furry carpet and large fluffy pillows. In the middle was a round plate of tasty morsels of food. Hiro was very grateful to see Kimba sprawled out contently on a huge red pillow, chewing on a piece of fish. Their mother sat next to her and rose up immediately when she saw Hiro and Griffin approaching.

"Ah, there you are," their mother said. "Welcome, Hiro. I'm grateful everything went smoothly." She looked from Hiro to her mate.

"Yes, no problems at all," he assured her.

"Excellent," she said, now looking to Hiro again. "Come and join us for a snack. Transfers always leave one famished. We have some tuna and some salmon and some trout. Springtime on Earth is just full of wonderful fishing."

Hiro curled up on a pillow next to Kimba. They locked eyes for a moment. Kimba twitched her whiskers, looked at Commander Griffin, looked back at Hiro, and tipped her head. She had figured it out too. Hiro nodded. *Yes, he's our father,* she thought.

"I hope you forgive me for not meeting you myself," their mother continued. "We came ahead to make sure the food was ready when you arrived. Commander Griffin stayed to wait for you to adjust. It's really quite a simple process. I hope you can see that now."

Kimba and Hiro both nodded. Hiro noticed that her sister's ears were almost white. No flush at all. She was clearly calm and at ease in this new and crazy situation.

"Since the humans are away for a few more days, we were hoping you would agree to stay for a while. You could get to know life on the ship a bit more," their mother said. "The time will come when this turn on Earth will be over. Then you will have to decide if you are ready to take your place here or if you want to go back."

She offered up some tidbits from the platter, and each of the sisters happily took a piece.

"Some cats," Griffin added, "go back and forth

for Earth-lives several times. Being placed in just the right circumstances on Earth as a house cat is like taking a vacation from life on the ship. That is how cats reaching the end of their full centuries of life sometimes choose to end their days. It's like what the humans call *retirement*."

"But life on Earth is not always so easy for a cat," their mother pointed out. "Many humans are kind and cherish their cats. Others do not. There are many, many cats on Earth who know nothing about where they come from. They don't realize they could have a better life. They live out a short, sad life on Earth, and that is the end of it. We help where we can, but it is not in the plan right now to change the order of things."

"So you never really intended to make a huge invasion and take over everything from the humans," Kimba said between bites of food.

"We consider this option every few decades or so," Mother said. "We rally the troops on Earth and see if there is really an interest in totally running the show."

"You said the Facebook plan was a test."

"Yes, it was. It was a test of the loyalty of each agent cat involved. But it was also a test to see how much cats on Earth want to take over. If the humans have gotten so out of line that cats no longer want to cohabitate with them, well, then something must be done."

"But most of them didn't cooperate and follow through with the plan, right?" Hiro said.

"Correct, Hiro. It was a total failure," she said.

"That let us know the majority of cats appreciate their humans and it is not yet time for an invasion," Griffin added.

"But there may still be a time?" Kimba asked.

"As I said, the High Council Leaders reconsider the idea every so often," Mother said.

They all nibbled on the tender bits of fish in silence for a few minutes. It was the most delicious thing Hiro had ever tasted. She locked eyes with Kimba, and her sister blinked her eyes slowly in delight.

"Would you like to see the rest of the ship?" Mother asked.

"Oh, yes!" Kimba answered immediately, her mouth still full of fish.

"Wonderful. There is no way we can see the whole thing during this visit, but we can give you the basic tour. I have arranged a room for you while you are with us. It is not as nice as what you would have if you lived here full time, but it will do to make sure you stay rested. We work in four-hour shifts. No cat can be expected to stay alert any longer than that."

With the platter of food soon gone, the four of them left the dining hall and took a leisurely tour of the more interesting parts of the ship.

The sisters were in awe of how enormous it all was. The walkways on the outer portions of the ship were impressive. One side was a giant wall of windows that looked out into the vastness of space. Stars twinkled in the blackness. Mother showed them a round, bluish ball in the distance. She said it was Earth.

"We hide out here among the meteors," she said, "but we are always close enough to make contact with our agents."

Kimba gazed at Earth in the distance and thought those windows were the best part of the whole ship. Staring out into space just made Hiro dizzy. Mother suggested she look away and walk closer to the inside wall.

"It can take some getting used to," she assured her.

They saw meeting rooms and sleeping quarters and more control rooms. Every time they entered a room, the cats they encountered were very impressed to meet them. They would lower their heads in a bow and keep their eyes down to avoid direct contact. Hiro found it very unnerving, but it did make sense.

They were special. Hiro had to face it. Nothing had made her feel the full impact of the importance of Kimba's and her destiny more than the way the cats on the ship reacted to them and their parents. All of the cats on the ship were very sure of who Kimba and Hiro were, even if they couldn't fully grasp it themselves.

We are the daughters of the high commander, Hiro had to remind herself.

At the end of the tour, their parents left them in a small but comfortable room. In one corner was a fountain of running water with a basin at the bottom, so there was always fresh water to drink. The floor was littered with blankets and soft pillows. It was perfect for a much-needed nap.

Hiro curled up near her sister. She could feel the hum of the ship's engines vibrating through the floor. As they each took a moment to groom and clean up before bed, Hiro wondered if that noise might keep her awake.

Her answer was soon evident. Both sisters were sound asleep before they finished their baths.

15

BEHIND THE SCENES

The next day, Hiro and Kimba enjoyed touring all around the enormous ship. Everywhere they went, the other cats gawked at them. Hiro even saw a few of them whisper to each other as they passed. It was an odd feeling, to be so closely observed by thousands of cats she had never seen before.

Their mother took them back to the main control room to visit Artemis and look through his computer into their very own bathroom nursery. That was even odder than the staring cats. The bathroom was empty and quiet. It was

158

amazing to see how the mirrors and the monitoring worked.

"Do you sit here all day?" Hiro asked Artemis.

"That would be impossible and not really necessary. I do four-hour shifts, but other secondary agents take shifts too. If something important happens, or if you try to make contact, the agent on duty will call me in my sleeping quarters. I can take over from the computer monitor in my room."

"So we could be waking you up when we try to communicate?" Kimba asked.

"That is possible, but you should never worry about that. It is part of my job."

Next, the sisters had a visit with the High Council Leaders. They met with the group in a large room filled with pillows and computer screens. It was all very formal.

The high commander introduced every Leader of the High Council, but Hiro knew she would never be able to remember any of their names. There were tabby cats and fluffy white cats and black cats and cats with faces so flat they looked like they had no noses at all.

Despite their varied appearance, each Leader expressed a solemn dignity and poise. They spoke calmly and quietly. Hiro and Kimba answered their questions about life in their human home on Earth and about their visit to the ship. The sisters tried to be as polite and proper as they could.

"So, you are well cared for and well fed?" a silver tabby asked.

"Yes, ma'am," Kimba said.

"I understand you have a very unique bond with the human male," a Leader with long blue-black fur said to Hiro.

"Yes, sir," she answered. "He takes very good care of me." *He's my Daddy,* she thought to herself.

Some of the Council members whispered to each other.

"We hope you can continue that bond during your time on Earth," he said. "There is much that can be learned through harmonious cohabitation."

"Yes, sir," Hiro said.

Hiro sensed these cats were all very old and

had seen many things in their lives. She wanted to ask how many of them had spent time on Earth, but somehow it seemed a bit brazen to start a conversation with any of those serious faces.

When the questions were all done, they headed back to the dining hall. Their father had a large platter of bits of fish and chicken sent over to them. He had business to attend to, so he left them with their mother.

"It must take a lot of work to run such a big ship with so many cats to worry about," Kimba said, watching him go.

"Yes," their mother agreed. "And even more so these days as some of our citizens feel the need to fight every decision I make and vie for personal power. Things have gotten very messy in the last few hundred years."

"How old are you?" Hiro asked in awe.

"Well," she answered, "we don't really keep track the way your humans do. I have been high commander for about two hundred Earth years, and I was in training with my own mother for many years before that."

"Wow," Hiro said looking at Kimba, who nodded in agreement, her mouth full of salmon.

"I told you, your time on Earth is only a part of your life. Your destiny is much larger and fuller than that. The time will come when I will need you to begin to learn more about this part of your life and your responsibilities here on the ship."

The three of them ate in silence for a while. Hiro noticed that the other cats in the room were pretending not to stare. They would glance her way and then drop their eyes the moment she noticed them. Everyone looked friendly enough, but she wondered how many of them were part of the group that was causing her mother so much trouble.

"Is one of us expected to be high commander one day?" Kimba finally whispered.

Hiro was stunned. She hadn't even considered that possibility.

"I have children much older than you two who have spent their lives on the ship. One of them will most likely be selected to take my place when the time comes. The job often goes to the oldest, but not always. Many assistant commanders are needed, and everyone has a role to fill."

Kimba nodded. Hiro wondered if that answer made her happy or sad. Kimba might love being high commander.

"Seats on the High Council are often filled with members of our family too," she continued. "Your experiences on Earth and bonding with humans will be useful there, most certainly."

Hiro liked that idea. She was uncomfortable with all of the focused interest from the cats on the ship. A behind-the-scenes role sounded much better. Mostly, she was just glad all of that was many, many years away.

"We should give you two a chance to rest," Felicity said. "It has been a busy morning full of much excitement."

Hiro was starting to feel the strain of being alert and paying attention for many hours. It was heightened by the effects of a full tummy. A nap sounded perfect.

The high commander led them back to the

same sleeping quarters from the night before
and wished them sweet dreams.

16

OPERATION
BROAD DAYLIGHT

om?" Mama said, "I can barely hear you. It's really windy today." Mama tried to aim her body so the wind would not hit the cell phone so directly.

"I'm here," Grandma answered from the yellow phone in her living room.

She paused the show on the TV and adjusted her position in her favorite big pink chair, pulling the springy coiled phone cord closer.

"Is everything going okay there?" Mama asked.

"Yes, yes," she assured her daughter, "the house is fine."

"What about the cats?"

"Ask her if she has seen Hiro yet," Daddy urged.

"I guess they are fine. They all hide when I come in, except for Kimba. She follows me around like a bossy supervisor."

Mama laughed at that image. Kimba was the only cat to run toward the door when strangers arrived. Her Kimba Baby had no fear.

"I didn't see Kimba yesterday, but I'm sure she was just asleep somewhere," Grandma said.

"And Buddy is there every time you come?"

"Yes, Buddy is there. He is waiting in the shrubs for me every day, just like clockwork. He marches right out for his dinner."

"Oh good," Mama sighed. "I'm so worried he will wander off again without us there to pay some attention to him. He was lost for over a year after we moved there."

"I know, I remember," Grandma said. "I try to come at the same time every day so he doesn't feel forgotten about. He even lets me scratch behind his ears a bit, and he rubs on my legs. He's doing just fine."

"What about Hiro?" Daddy whispered insistently.

"What about Hiro?" Mama asked, nodding and waving him away with a smile. "Have you seen her yet?"

"No," Grandma said. "She hides from me the whole time."

"Her daddy is very worried about her," Mama said with a chuckle. "I know it's hard for you, but when you go by this evening, would you please look under the bed in our room and at least see if she is there? It will calm his nerves."

"Okay, fine," Grandma said. "I'll try to make eye contact with her."

"Thanks, Mom."

"How's the weather there?"

"Oh, it's beautiful today. The girls are collecting sea shells, and their daddy helped them make a sandcastle kingdom. He's the king, of course."

"Of course," Grandma said. "Well, you all stay safe and have a good time."

"We will. See you soon."

"Bye," Grandma said.

She hung up the phone, took a long swig of Pepsi from the large glass next to her, and turned the TV back on. She had another hour or so before she needed to make her daily visit.

They sure do worry a lot about those cats, she thought.

She did not look forward to trying to find Hiro that evening. That cat could hide really well.

From the undergrowth next to the beach, Tsunami and Typhoon listened to the phone call in horrified shock. They had been informed that the last phase of the operation was in progress and the sisters were now on the home ship. What would happen when the human grandmother went looking for Hiro and couldn't find her?

They shouldn't dare make a report until after

all of the humans were asleep, but it was imperative they warn Artemis right away. Hiro needed to be exactly where she was supposed to be or there would be no explanation for where she had gone. The human male might be so upset that he would head home early. There would certainly be a disruption in the normal chain of human events. That was unacceptable.

Unusual steps would need to be taken.

Typhoon stayed on guard, and Tsunami raced around to the front of the building. Dashing into the undergrowth near the parking garage, she nearly collided with Hurricane as she sat on her watch duty. Thunder dozed nearby.

"What's happening?" Hurricane asked.

"We overheard a phone conversation with the grandmother. The human male is worried that she has not seen Hiro since they left. He was very insistent that she make contact with Hiro today to be sure she is okay."

"But . . . Hiro is on the ship right now."

"Yes," Tsunami hissed, "I know. That's why I'm running!"

"We were worried about them heading home early, but we never anticipated this. It is imperative to all missions that the humans never notice anything out of place or unusual."

"I am aware of the guidelines for every mission," Tsunami said with a grumble.

"But I don't see how we can avoid a security breach now. When is the grandmother going to check for Hiro?"

"They were not specific, but they said 'this evening.'"

"That could mean anything!"

Tsunami and Hurricane faced each other, each knowing what needed to be done but neither willing to say it out loud. Thunder was roused by the urgency of their voices. One look at the thrashing stump of Tsunami's tail, and he knew there was a problem.

"What's going on?" he asked.

"We need to implement Operation Broad Daylight," Hurricane said.

"What? It can't be that desperate, can it?" Thunder said, looking at his partner.

"Yes, it absolutely is," Hurricane answered, her eyes fully dilated and her ears perked and alert.

Thunder bristled his whiskers. His tail thrashed as he pondered how to proceed.

"We don't have any choice," Hurricane said. "Tsunami and I will take care of it. You stay here and watch for any other activity."

"Be careful," Thunder whispered.

There was no safe way to make contact during the day, but an emergency plan had been put into place many years ago. No one had ever attempted it, until now. Moving urgently, Tsunami and Hurricane slunk along the side of the building toward the swimming pool.

A full conversation through the large mirror in the open shower area was out of the question. There was not enough time to give a warning, and far too many people were out and about. The beach agents agreed that the long-unused plan for the public bathroom was the only choice.

Hurricane tiptoed her way along through the undergrowth until she reached the beach shower. The area was temporarily clear of humans. They were all in the pool or enjoying the ocean. Watching from the sidewalk, Tsunami chirped the "all clear." Hurricane faced the mirror and spoke as loudly as she dared.

"This is agent Hurricane, requesting special communications via Operation Broad Daylight. I repeat—This is agent Hurricane, requesting special communications via Operation Broad Daylight."

She knew no agent would appear in the mirror and risk being discovered, but she hoped whoever was monitoring the situation was paying attention and would follow the protocol. A lazy or inattentive agent could blow the whole operation. Hurricane rejoined Tsunami in the bushes, and the two agents anticipated their opportunity.

Watching from the cover of the nearby shrubs, the cats waited for several minutes until the group in the girls' bathroom emerged. For the moment, the area was now empty.

Hurricane slipped quietly into the bathroom, and Tsunami took a lookout position at the doorway. She might only have a second or two to give a warning if a human approached. There was no time to waste.

After checking the bathroom to be sure the coast was clear, Hurricane jumped onto a sink and looked hopefully into the small metal-framed mirror.

"Greetings," she whispered. "Is anyone there?"

The image of Artemis appeared in the mirror. Sensing the severity of the situation, the agent on watch had summoned him. The beach agents were not known for overreacting. So, despite the risk, Artemis acted on good faith that vital information needed to be shared and opened a window for communication.

"Yes, what is so important that you need to report it at this moment?"

"We overheard the human female ask the grandmother to specifically find Hiro and make sure she is okay. The male is becoming concerned the grandmother has not seen his cat since they left. We believe if the grandmother cannot find Hiro, there will be great drama from the human male. It would lead to a definite interference in the normal chain of human activities. He might

173

even insist they return home immediately."

"Understood. I will pass on this information to the high commander at once. Good work, Agent Hurricane. Well done."

A sharp meow echoed from the doorway and bounced off the bright-blue walls of the bathroom.

"Oooo, look at the kitty!" A little girl's voice carried into the concrete room. "She's got a funny little tail!"

The image in the mirror vanished. Hurricane sighed in relief and jumped down from the sink. She had done her duty. She knew the message had been delivered. They had not been caught communicating. Now she and Tsunami just needed to escape.

Hurricane peeked out of the large bathroom doorway and saw Tsunami enduring the petting and attentions of two small girls in very frilly pink bathing suits.

What a devoted agent, she thought, knowing what torture it must be to let herself be mauled in such a manner.

"Look, there's another one!" One of the little girls screamed, preparing to rush toward Hurricane. "Look at her beautiful swirly fur!"

"Girls!" a woman shouted across the pool deck. "Leave those cats alone! They are strays and could have all kinds of diseases."

"Awww, Mom," the girls both whined.

It was enough of a window of opportunity, and the cats took it. They dashed into the nearby bushes and buried themselves deep in the under-growth.

"Full of diseases?" Hurricane huffed.

"Were you able to complete the message?" Tsunami asked.

"Yes," she said. "Thank you for doing what was necessary to delay those children from entering the bathroom."

"That's my job," she said firmly. "But I definitely need a bath now. Who knows what was on their hands."

The sandcastle kingdom Daddy built
on Cocoa Beach.

17

HOME AGAIN

Hiro was roused by her mother's voice. She opened one eye and saw Kimba already sitting up next to her, ears pink and alert.

"Hiro," Mother said urgently, "you need to wake up."

The tone of her mother's voice and the look on her sister's face were enough to bring Hiro to her senses quickly.

"We need to transfer you back down to the house right away."

"I thought we got to stay for a while longer?" Kimba said sadly.

"That was my hope too, My Daughter, but there has been a change in the situation."

"Is Daddy okay?" Hiro worried.

"He is fine," she assured her, "but he is concerned about the fact that the grandmother has not seen you since they left. He has asked her to look for you and let him know you are okay."

Hiro felt all warm inside, knowing Daddy was worried about her. But she also realized what might happen if Grandma couldn't find her. Daddy would be beside himself. She stretched as quickly as she could and then followed her mother and a disgruntled Kimba into the hallway. Griffin met them there.

"Everything is being prepared for the transfer," he said firmly.

"Good," their Mother said. "There is no time to lose."

The four of them trotted quickly down the long hallway, thousands of stars twinkling at them from the windows. Kimba glanced out longingly, but Hiro kept her eyes straight ahead. She couldn't risk feeling out of sorts now.

At the doors of the communications room, special agents were waiting to escort them through the area. All eyes followed them again as they made their way quickly to the platform in the middle.

A white cat with fluffy fur and a flat face greeted them. His bright-green eyes were focused and intent.

"Artemis says he can see the grandmother's car already in the driveway," the white cat informed the high commander.

"How can he see that?" Kimba asked.

"We have a monitor that reflects through the car window of the older human girl," Griffin said. "It is how we communicate with your uncle."

"Our uncle?" Hiro said, but their mother immediately distracted them.

"You must focus and prepare," she said firmly. "Hiro is the one she will be looking for. She must go first."

Hiro swallowed hard, but she knew the high commander was right. She trotted up the steps onto the platform and tried to calm herself down. They had raced to get there, and it was all very stressful.

Breathe, she thought. *Be calm.*

"Her heart rate is too fast," the white cat at the controls said. "You need to help her relax."

Kimba looked at her mother, not sure what to do. In a swift movement, their mother climbed onto the platform and leaned in close to her little black-and-white daughter. In that moment, she was not the high commander preparing an agent for transfer. She was simply a mother who needed to keep her daughter safe.

Rubbing the top of her head against Hiro's, Felicity purred gently to her. It was the first time her mother had touched her. There was a warmth to that contact that took Hiro by surprise.

"Everything will be fine," Hiro's mother whispered in her ear. "In just a few moments you will be safely back in your nursery room. You will make contact with the grandmother, she will tell the daddy, and that will be the end of it."

Hiro felt her whole body relax in an instinctive response to her mother's attention. A deep purr vibrated up from her own throat as well. Her heart rate slowed, and every inch of her body felt calm and at ease.

"Artemis says the bathroom is still clear," the white cat said. "We are ready."

"Now relax and let yourself go," Felicity said. "Count to ten, and it will be done."

Then she stepped out of the way.

Hiro glanced at Kimba, who nodded encouragingly. She looked at her mother and her father. Then she closed her eyes and thought of home and Daddy. The tingling started along her spine, and she saw the bright light, even through closed eyelids.

Daddy . . . Daddy . . . Daddy, she whispered to herself.

Then she felt the cold tile of the bathroom floor under her feet. The light faded, and she was home.

She had barely opened her eyes when she

heard Grandma calling from the living room. Before she could decide how to respond, Grandma came into the bedroom and spotted her through the bathroom door.

"Well, there you are," she said in a high-pitched, sing-song voice that sounded rather like Mama's. "I didn't even have to go searching."

Hiro blinked at her slowly and then darted under the bed. There was no way she was letting Grandma pick her up. Their caretaker did not seem the least bit bothered by this.

"Such a fuss over nothing," she said.

After running some fresh water in the tub, Grandma headed home without looking back.

Once she heard the deadbolt on the front door click into place, Hiro ventured out from under the bed. She peeked into the bathroom, but Kimba was not there.

"Artemis?" Hiro called out. "Where's Kimba?"

His image appeared in the mirror.

"She will be along in a moment. We wanted to wait until we were sure the grandmother was

182

gone. Please stand back out of the way so there's no interference."

Hiro stepped back from the door, and in a moment Kimba appeared in the middle of the bathroom floor. After pausing for another minute to let her sister get her bearings, Hiro approached and rubbed along her sister's side.

"I thought you might not come back," Hiro whispered.

"I thought I might not too," Kimba admitted. "But they didn't ask me to stay."

"Mama would have been terribly sad. She would miss you very much."

"I know. I would miss all of you too. Mother said we can come back another time, and someday we will have to choose between living on Earth or living on the ship."

"She means after we get old on Earth."

"Yes."

"Well, that's a long time away from now." Hiro sighed gratefully.

It was good to be home. She jumped into the

tub in one leap and gratefully drank from the puddle of water Grandma had poured for her. The large bowl of crunchy cat food was not the same as the tidbits of fish on the spaceship, but it tasted like home and love and family.

That had been a grand adventure, but all Hiro wanted now was for Daddy to come home and for her life to get back to normal.

Griffin and Felicity sat together near the transfer platform for several minutes after their daughters had returned to Earth.

"They didn't stay to visit as long as we had hoped," Griffin finally said, "but at least now they have seen the ship and will believe us about their heritage and the importance of their destiny."

"And they won't be afraid to make a transfer quickly if they are ever in danger," Felicity added. Then she sighed.

It was hard letting them go back to the human household, where she had so little control over their lives. It was not unusual for her children to spend time on Earth. It was a wonderful training ground for everything being part of the High Command would demand of them later in life. But somehow, with these two, it tugged at her heart more. She had grown old, even for a cat, and had not ever expected to have these two daughters. They were certainly the last of her children.

"You can check on them every day," Griffin said quietly.

"I know. And Artemis will let us know immediately if there is ever a problem."

"My brother is right there too. He will stand guard for a while longer, until they are old enough to fend for themselves better. So there's nothing to worry about."

Felicity didn't know how to explain to her mate that she wasn't exactly worried. She was sad. But there was no time to dwell on it. The High Council would meet soon to discuss how best to deal with the increasingly rebellious behavior of small factions of cats on the ship.

For the high commander, there was no time for sentimental feelings. She stiffened her whiskers, perked her ears up tall, and stalked out of the communications room. Griffin followed his mate, ready to support her leadership, no matter what the cost.

18

WAITING

Being back in the quiet of the house was a bit of a shock after spending so much time surrounded by thousands of cats. Hiro didn't normally feel the need for any company but Daddy. But now, in the silence of the bedroom, she began to wonder what it would be like to live on the ship all the time. There would be a cat or two or more around every corner, and they all tended to stare at her. Maybe all of that gawking would wear off after a while. But what if it didn't?

Quiet is better, she thought.

She loved her Earth house and the big bed to hide under and drinks from the bathtub. And Daddy, of course.

Home is better.

Asleep in her bed high up on Mama's bookshelf, Kimba struggled with an emptiness in her heart. Even Mama coming home and making a fuss over how beautiful she was wouldn't fill the void. She knew Hiro couldn't understand, but Kimba missed the ship very much.

Following along next to her mother, the high commander, Kimba had felt excited and important. A tingle ran along her spine and all the way out the tips of her toes at the memory of it. She flexed her claws in and out, enjoying every last bit of that electric, powerful feeling.

There were not many things in her young life that Kimba was 100% sure of, but she was absolutely certain she would return to that spaceship. The white cat knew it with every hair on her body. When the time came, she would be ready.

After they had both enjoyed a long night's sleep,

Kimba sauntered into the bedroom to check on her sister. She discovered her sleeping up on top of the bed, instead of hiding under it. Maybe after being on the ship and meeting Artemis and their parents face-to-face, there was less to be afraid of.

Kimba jumped lightly up onto the bed, and Hiro raised her head sleepily to greet her. Kimba licked the top of her sister's head three times and then plopped down next to her. There was not much to do today except wait for the family to come home.

"That trip to the ship really wore me out," Kimba said, stretching out long and then rolling onto her back. "It's more excitement than we have had in a year around here."

"I feel like I could sleep for a week." Hiro sighed. "I'm glad we went, but it's even nicer to be back home."

Kimba didn't really agree, but she kept quiet. There was no point in making her sister nervous. Kimba would stay there on Earth and bide her time. Someday, Mother would call for them.

"Do you miss anything about the ship?" Kimba asked her sleepy sister.

"Mmmm," Hiro thought dreamily, "the food."

"Ooohhh," Kimba sighed. "Those bits of fish were extra good."

"We'll have to watch for a chance to sneak some from the plate the next time Mindy or Leia has the food that smells like that."

"Maybe if we make big, sad eyes," Kimba added.

"Or let them pick us up and cuddle."

Yeesh, Kimba thought. She wasn't sure she wanted the fish that badly.

"Do you think we should make some kind of report to Artemis?" Hiro wondered.

"I don't know," Kimba said. "Everything happened so quickly at the end there that Mother didn't say what we should do next."

"Maybe in a little bit. I'm so tired."

"Okay," Kimba agreed and laid her head down on the bed.

In a moment, they were both fast asleep again.

Grandma's arrival later in the day woke the sleeping sisters. Kimba jumped down to investigate at the first sounds from the front door, but Hiro was too groggy to run away.

"Well, there you are, right in the middle of the bed after all of that fuss yesterday." Grandma laughed.

She poured fresh water in the tub for Hiro and was quickly gone.

The temptation of a drink of water was enough to get Hiro up and off the bed. She peered around the corner into the bathroom, but it was all quiet inside. There really wasn't any reason to be scared of going in now. She knew someone was watching, but there was no longer any fear of the Cats in the Mirror.

She jumped into the tub and got some water. Then she visited the litter box and crunched her way through a bit of the dry food. The mirror was quiet. If Artemis was watching, he didn't say anything.

With nothing much else to do, Hiro wandered back out into the bedroom and jumped up onto the window ledge to watch the birds playing in the bushes. Glancing up at the sky, she knew her mother and her father, and Artemis and Regalus, and all of those other cats were up there somewhere.

The Cat in the Mirror had been right. Once you know something big and important like that, you can never *unknow* it. The sisters would never think about their world the same way again.

Hiro, bird-watching from the
window with Kimba.

19

DADDY IS HOME

Hiro was asleep, curled up on the big bed all by herself, when the familiar rumbling of the garage door instinctively roused her. That noise meant Daddy was home from work. Her mind was trained to wake up at the first grinding and humming noises so she could run to greet him. Lifting her head sleepily, she wondered if she had simply dreamt that happy sound, like so many others over the week. Then she heard faint voices and the slamming of car doors.

Without a single stretch, Hiro leapt from the

bed, landing stiffly on the bedroom floor. She peeked out of the door and saw Kimba already sitting in the middle of the living room. Her ears twitched and turned, trying to hear what was happening. Hiro looked toward the door to the garage too, her heart beating so fast she could barely breathe.

Then the door opened, and Mindy and Leia burst in. Their faces were red and burnt from the sun, hair unkempt and windblown.

"Kimba!" Leia shrieked, charging over to grab the white cat.

Kimba quickly ran to hide behind the books on the living room shelf to avoid a squishing.

"Sheesh, give the poor thing a break," Mindy said. "She's probably mad at us for leaving her alone so long."

"No, she's not mad. She missed us," Leia insisted, trying to find a way to get to Kimba.

The sleek white cat was an expert hider, so the girl didn't stand a chance. Leia was quickly distracted by thoughts of her own cat.

"Miss Fatty Cat?" she called. "Where arrre yooou?"

Leia raced up the stairs to look for her.

Hiro watched quietly, out of sight in the bedroom. If the girls were here, Daddy couldn't be far behind.

He must be here!! she thought, dizzy with excitement.

Mama was the next one through the door, toting several large bags and looking flustered.

"Girls!" she called out. "Get your stuff out of the car! Don't just leave it for us to deal with!"

She sighed and put the bags down in a corner of the kitchen.

"Honey, grab the suitcases first," she called back to the garage.

Honey? That's what Mama calls him. My Daddy!

"Okay," a familiar voice called from the garage, "but the girls need to come help."

I can hear him! He is out there!

She wanted to run to him and tell him how

much she had missed him. But with so much activity and piles of bags and tromping feet, it was scary to run right out into the middle of it.

He will come and find me. I know he will, she thought.

Hiro restrained herself and waited at the bedroom door, but her heart felt like it was going to burst.

Then he was inside the house. She could see him. His face was a darker brown, and he looked tired, but he was there.

Daddy.

He set down the suitcases he had dragged into the house and sighed deeply.

"Ah, good to be home," he said, smiling at Mama. Then he paused and looked around the living room.

"Oh, go find her," Mama said, laughing. "I'm sure she's fine, but you're not going to be satisfied until you see for yourself."

Daddy gave her a big hug and then headed for the bedroom. Hiro ducked around back into the room and sat down next to the dresser, where he would be sure to see her but no one else would.

"Hiro?" he called, looking around the bedroom.

Then he spotted her. Her heart jumped, and a huge, warm smile spread across his face.

"There you are. Hey, baby, how are you? Did you miss me? Did you sleep okay without me?" he said as he bent down to pick her up.

Hiro knew she was supposed to be cool and aloof and a bit angry with him for leaving her behind, but she couldn't do it. A pathetic *meerooow* of relief burst out, and purrs suddenly vibrated through her whole body.

Daddy lifted her up on his shoulder. She arched her back and rubbed the top of her head against his furry face. He kissed the white stripe that ran up her nose and cooed at her about how beautiful she was.

Daddy's home. My Daddy.

All thoughts of spaceships and family duty washed away under the glow of his love and attention. He smelled funny, like a hundred different people and places she couldn't recognize. But when she cuddled in close and nuzzled into his neck, she could still find that warm, special scent that reminded her of love and home. Her Daddy. He was safe.

Still holding her in his arms, Daddy flopped down on the bed and propped her up on his chest. Just like they did every night of her life, Hiro bunted against Daddy's face, and he gave her head gentle kisses with every bunt. She wasn't sure if Artemis could see from the mirror, but she didn't really care. Daddy was back.

"Did you miss me while I was on vacation?" he asked her.

Oh yes, she chortled to him and then sat on his chest and stared him in the face. *I had a vacation of my own,* she thought. *But I went even farther away than you did. I went so far away, I can't even imagine it.*

"Vacations are nice," Daddy said, "but it's always the very best to come back home again."

Hiro blinked slowly at him in agreement.

Home is the very best.

Hiro and Daddy, enjoying some snuggle time.
She's resting her head on his hand.

20
BACK TO NORMAL

The routine of family life started up again very quickly the next morning. Once the girls were off to school, Mama started on the piles of laundry that she emptied out of the suitcases. Hiro and Kimba climbed over the mounds and investigated all of the odd smells.

The big pool towels were covered with a grit that smelled like old fish. Kimba rolled around in them, loving the odor. The one thing they didn't smell on the clothes was other cats. That made Hiro very happy.

While the laundry was washing, Mama left in the car for a while and returned with The Big Black Beast. He burst through the door from the garage, waggling from head to toe and drooling everywhere. Immediately sticking his nose in the pile of dirty beach towels, he sniffed and slobbered.

"How's that smell?" Mama asked him.

The Beast pulled his nose out of the towels and sneezed.

Snerk.

"That good, huh?" She laughed.

He then set about smelling every inch of the house, as fast as he could, to make sure everything was in order.

As The Beast snuffled his way into the bedroom, he stopped at the end of the big grown-up bed, where Hiro was trying to get a nap. He plopped his enormous head down a few feet away from her and gave her several sniffily tests. Hiro held her ground, but her whole body tensed. The fur along her back ridge rose, ready to be impressive if necessary.

"You smell funny," The Beast said hoarsely.

Can he smell the spaceship on my fur?

Hiro didn't think it smelled different, but then she was not The Beast with his super-sniffer.

"I took a little trip while you were gone."

"Oh, okay. It smells better than the place where I was," he said.

"Where were you?" Hiro asked, noticing The Beast smelled like shampoo instead of his normal, awful, what-I-rolled-in-yesterday odor. His voice sounded odd too, like he could barely get his words out.

"The same place I always go when the suitcases come out," he said sadly. "It's like being in my cage, but it's bigger. There are lots of other dogs in other cages too. Everyone barks all the time. They let me out to play a couple of times a day and give me bones to chew, but it's pretty boring."

"What's wrong with your voice?" she asked.

The Beast tried to clear his throat, but all that came out was a nasty retching sound.

"Barking louder than all the other dogs for

203

days and days is hard on the throat," he finally gurgled.

With that, he took a moment to investigate the bathroom and the suitcases in there. Then he snuffled his way back out into the living room.

Why is it necessary to bark louder than the other dogs all day? Hiro wondered. *Silly Beast.*

After school, Mindy pulled her car up into the driveway, instead of leaving it in front of the house. She unrolled the garden hose and sprayed water all over the hood of her car.

Hiro and Kimba had been keeping Mama company in the office while she worked on the computer. It was nice to breathe the fresh air through the open windows. Birds playing and splashing in the big white birdbath was interesting enough, but they were fascinated by this new development. Daddy washed his fancy sports car all the time, but Mindy was never so industrious with her little car.

"What inspired all of this desire to clean?" Mama laughed, calling through the open window in her office.

"It looks like Buddy had a party on the hood of my car while we were gone," Mindy said, half annoyed and half laughing. "There are cat prints everywhere!"

"That should wash off pretty easily," Mama said.

She scratched Kimba gently on the top of the head. Kimba gazed up at her and slowly blinked her eyes. Even the independent white cat had to admit that it was nice to have things back to normal.

"Looks like you came through it all just fine, Miss Kimba," Mama said. "One blue eye and one green eye. Just as it should be."

Mama gave her a quick scritchy-scratch on the back and then sat down at the computer again. Kimba just yawned and focused back out the window.

Just as it should be for a long, long time, she thought.

Mindy had returned to tackling the car hood with a soapy sponge and more water. It provided some entertainment for the feline sisters.

When Daddy arrived home from work that day, he gathered the family in the living room. From their spots in Mama's office, Kimba and Hiro heard the girls come thundering down the stairs. Kimba's ears twitched forward at full attention.

"He's got a gift bag with him," Kimba said, jumping down from high up on Mama's bookshelf. "I can hear it crinkling."

A gift bag was always enticing. The white tissue paper inside was fantastic for ripping and shredding.

"Today is a very special day," Daddy announced. "Ah, good, the babies have joined us." He seemed pleased that Hiro and Kimba had come into the room.

Kimba stopped in her tracks and pretended her front foot needed grooming immediately. She couldn't possibly let on that she had come rushing into the room on purpose. Hiro didn't like those games. She hopped up on a little table next to the big comfy sofa and waited to see what was so special about today.

"Today," he continued dramatically, "is Hiro and Kimba's birthday!"

Leia clapped her hands and cheered. Mindy reached over and stroked Hiro's head.

"They must be two years old," she said. "How old is that in people years?"

"That would make them about nine or ten, I suppose," Mama said. "Everyone figures it a bit differently. Cats can live a long time. Remember Aunt Jennie's cat Showboat? He lived to be twenty-two years old. Our baby kittens are just getting started."

You don't know the half of it, Hiro thought. She looked over at Kimba, and the two shared a knowing wink. They had hundreds of years ahead of them.

"I think it's really fun that we know for sure when they were born," Daddy said. "Miss Fatty Cat and Slinky were born some time in September, based on what the rescue group said. And we have no idea when Buddy was born, just a rough idea of how old he is from what the vet

207

says. But not our babies. They were just a day or so old when we found them, so we can make a pretty good guess that today, April 18th, is their birthday."

"And what have you got in that bag?" Mama asked.

"Well, a present for them, of course."

Daddy pulled a long black stick out of the bag. At the end was a rubbery string with four colorful feathers attached to the tip. Without hesitation, Kimba launched herself into the air, claws splayed and ready for the kill. She landed firmly on the sofa between the girls, the feathers under her belly and at her mercy. The victim received a toss and a roll, terrible bites from her deadly jaws, and many kicks by her strong back feet, but the feathers held on tight. The girls squealed in delight.

Hiro blinked up at Daddy. She didn't like leaping around in front of the whole family. She preferred private time to hide under the bed while Daddy dangled a toy just over the edge for her to bat at.

We can play together later, when we are alone, she thought.

"Can we have a chocolate cake to celebrate?" Leia asked.

"The kittens can't eat chocolate." Mama laughed.

"No, but I can," Leia said with a grin.

"Let me see what I have in the pantry," Mama said, getting up to look. "I usually keep a box of something like that around, just in case."

"Yellow cake with chocolate frosting," Mindy called after her, winking at Daddy because she knew it was his favorite.

"Oooo." He smiled, pulling on the end of the toy and sending Kimba into another round of attack. "I could eat some yellow cake with chocolate frosting."

"I'm sure you could," Mama said from the pantry. "Good thing I have a box of mix and a tub of frosting. Flat or layers?" she asked.

"Flat," Leia yelled quickly. "You get more frosting that way."

"Flat it is," Mama said and pulled out the mixer from the bottom cabinet.

The girls wandered into the kitchen to help

209

and to be sure they were handy to lick the mixing bowl. Daddy gave up the toy to Kimba, who promptly ran with it into the dining room and under the big table. Then he sat down on the sofa next to Hiro.

"How's my favorite girl today?" he asked her. "Can I get some kisses?"

Hiro leaned in close and rubbed the top of her head against Daddy's furry face. He gave her kisses on the flat part between her ears. Then Daddy sighed, put up the foot rest on the sofa, and turned on the TV.

The girls had left a box of cheese crackers on the table from their after-school snack. Hiro's favorite. It was the one bit of "people food" Daddy always shared with her. When Daddy didn't immediately open the box, Hiro casually rubbed her head along the side. Then she bumped his shoulder with her head and rubbed on the box again. Daddy caught on quickly.

"Okay, okay." He laughed. "I suppose we can have a couple before dinner."

The delightful sound of crinkly wrap inside

the box made Hiro start to drool a little bit. Daddy took out a couple of square crackers, broke them into smaller pieces, and piled them up on the table in front of Hiro. She hunkered down and gobbled them up, while Daddy popped a couple of crackers in his own mouth too.

The routine of daily life had been restored. Everything was just as it should be. The familiar sights and sounds of dinnertime came from the kitchen. Dishes clanked and drawers opened and shut. For The Beast, those sounds meant dinner for him too. He sat anxiously where Mama would be sure to see him, tail flopping violently against the floor.

"I think Max is ready for his D-I-N-N-E-R," Mindy spelled carefully, noticing his pose.

"Are you ready for . . . *dinner*?" Mama said in a baby voice, pulling a can of dog food from the pantry.

The Beast began to waggle from head to toe, like he would break in two. Whines trembled from deep in his throat. He didn't know much, but he knew "dinner."

"Are you sure?" Mama teased. "We can always wait until later."

Knowing his part of the game, The Beast spun in circles, nearly bashing his head on the corner of the kitchen table. He reared up on his back legs, trembling with whimpers.

"I suppose I should get . . . a *spoon*," Mama said dramatically, opening the silverware drawer and slowly pulling one out.

"Dinner! Dinner! Dinner!!" The Beast barked hoarsely.

Laughing at his antics, Mama headed out the back door with the can of dog food and the spoon. The Beast whined and barked and waggled right at her heels. Every night, just the same. Hiro was grateful to have the family routine back. It was safe and comforting and peaceful, even if it involved The Beast.

Spring Break had been an interesting week, that was for sure. Kimba and Hiro had finally learned about their space-traveling cat family. Artemis had been right. Visiting the ship and truly understanding their place in the universe would change them, and there was no going back. The sisters had a heritage of duty and honor and power and responsibility. They had a destiny that lies in the stars, and the time would come to fulfill it.

Someday, Artemis would call for them again. Someday, they would be expected to follow the high commander and assume their roles as her daughters. A trip to the ship wouldn't always just be a brief vacation. The reality of what the future must hold could not be denied.

But for now, the young cats were content to be with their human family. They could hide out on Earth with the people who made them feel loved and safe and secure. Life could go on from day to day, and the cats would be happy.

Of course, not much in this world stays the same for long.

Miss Fatty Cat leapt onto the counter in Leia's bathroom, facing the mirror. Everyone was occupied downstairs, so she could be sure of some privacy for a few minutes. Almost immediately, the image of a white long-haired cat with a flat face and bright-green eyes appeared in the mirror.

"Greetings, Agent Ebony," he said. "I'm surprised to be hearing from you again. Have you changed your mind about offering your services?"

"Yes," Miss Fatty Cat said in a low voice. "I can't take any more of those stupid cats being treated like God's gift to the family. They never should have come here."

"You must be very careful and not let them know what you are up to," the Cat in the Mirror said. "Their recent visit to the main ship will certainly help to stir up the opposition forces and gain us new members. I'm sure you can help us in our struggle for equality and power."

"Just tell me what to do," Miss Fatty Cat growled.

THE END

Don't miss Book 3 in the Cats in the Mirror series! Keep reading for a sample of Chapter 1.

Miss Fatty Cat's Revenge

NIGHTTIME SONG

Kimba, the stealthy hunter, crept between the sleeping bodies. Not one of them sensed her presence. Choosing the perfect victim, she took hold of his throat. She lifted her prey carefully so his cries did not wake the others. The tiny pig in the striped sweater was now helpless in her clutches. Kimba slipped away and began her victory song as she climbed the steep mountain to rejoin her family.

"I have won!" she sang loud and clear. "The victory is mine. The pig is dead. Hurrah for Kimba!"

217

"Yes, Kimba, we hear you. You are a mighty hunter," Mama mumbled from behind the bedroom door. "Now go back to sleep," she said.

Kimba dropped her prize outside the door and began washing her front toes in frustration. If Mama were really impressed, she would have opened the door to admire her Kimba Baby's hard work.

Humans just don't understand the skill it takes to be a master hunter, she thought sadly.

In the old house, it was a quick trip from the toy collection on Mama's office shelves to the bedroom door. In this new house, it now required lugging her victim up a tall staircase. Some appreciation would be nice. She sang a few extra forlorn notes, just to make sure Mama understood.

"Herrrow, herrrow, merrrrow!"

In the room next door, Miss Fatty Cat was snoring, belly-up on Leia's bed. Kimba's nightly routine disturbed her sleep, and she rolled onto her side with a loud snort. Leia groaned and pulled the blankets up over her head. All of the nighttime hunting and singing was nothing new, but Leia's room used to be far away from the adults. The girl and her fat cat slept through it. Not in this strange new house.

Stupid cat, sing while you can, Miss Fatty Cat thought. *Your time is coming.*

Special Agent Artemis paced back and forth outside the door of the High Council chamber. It had been over a week since Felicity's daughters had vanished without a trace. The new agent monitoring them during the daytime didn't understand what it meant when strange men took furniture from the bedroom. The packing was over before Artemis came back to his station.

Watching the video playback, Artemis felt a chill run along his spine. The family had moved, and he had no idea where to begin looking for the sisters who were supposed to be under his watchful eye. Kimba and Hiro were gone, but he would not rest until he found them.

End of Chapter 1 Sample

Don't miss out on the whole Cats in the Mirror series!

And the Companion Books
to the Series

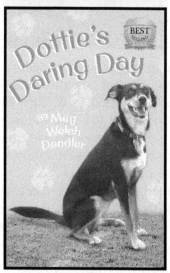

Also by Meg Welch Dendler

Best Juvenile Book 2018
Oklahoma Writers' Federation

Fire-breathing dragon in the kingdom! Princess
Bianca had never set foot outside the castle walls. Not
once in her over-protected, pink, fluffy life. But when
a dragon was spotted in the land and fear spread that
the monster had conquered the king and his brave
knights, Bianca realized it was her duty to protect her
kingdom. She will have to prove she can be braver
and stronger than anyone believed because the threat
outside the protection of her castle tower was more
dangerous and magical than she ever imagined.

"Princess Bianca rules, in every way!"
New England Children's Book Review

222

And for Grown-up Readers

Dead, but not gone. Penny had been stuck in the same
cozy diner for decades—ever since she died in 1952. Over
the years she served ice cream to those who stopped by
on their way to the next level of existence, helping to ease
their transition into The Light, a place she couldn't go. But
it didn't matter to Penny. She was safe and content. Then
ridiculously handsome bad boy biker Jake dropped in and
became stuck as well, turning her world upside down.
Should Penny fight to keep her afterlife the same,
or should she risk losing it all for a chance at love?

If you enjoyed Hiro's story, please take a moment to leave a review at Amazon.com or Goodreads.com and tell your friends!

Sign up for Meg's Reader's Group (at megdendler.com) to hear about new books, sales, and other exciting events in the lives of Kimba and her friends. You'll also get a free short story, "Sonya's Steps," about a rescued tiger.

AUTHOR'S NOTE

**If we ever needed to find Hiro,
we just opened a box of cheese crackers.**

When my family arrived in Cocoa Beach, Florida, in 2011, we immediately went out onto the balcony to enjoy the wonderful view of the ocean. There, on the ground below us, were two stray cats. We all quickly agreed that they were agents sent to monitor us while we were on vacation. The wheels in my head started spinning, and the basic storyline for *Vacation Hiro* was born.

As with award-winning *Why Kimba Saved The World*, there were many similarities to our real life mixed in with the alien cat adventures.

Grandma in this story was based on my real mother, who always lived close to us while the girls were growing up. In Houston, her house was just around the corner, and she was our only petsitter during vacations. Even though she was highly active with many different groups, I couldn't help but describe her in her favorite environment: her big pink chair, watching TV, with a large glass of Pepsi. She did eventually graduate to a cordless phone.

Felicity, the high commander, was inspired by a beautiful calico cat who lived up the street from us. We always wondered if she might be Kimba and Hiro's mother, but we never asked or learned her real name. Commander Griffin was based on my brother-in-law John's much-beloved cat. We joked that Griffin looked very much like our Buddy, but twice the size. Griffin was furry and puffy and more like a stuffed animal than a hunter. My sister says he would howl and cry when John left the house for work. Many cats miss their humans as much as any dog does, and don't let anyone convince you otherwise.

While Kimba was my cat (as much as she allowed herself to belong to anyone), Hiro belonged to my husband, also known as Daddy. Or maybe he belonged to her. Whichever way you look at it, there was a special light in their eyes that only went on between the two of them. I might have stalled on writing this book for a long time, but my husband just had to know how it would all turn out. He cried several times when he read the manuscript (and every time he reads a portion of the book), so I think I did well as far as he was concerned. Daddy has also made it perfectly clear that, in the next book, Hiro needs to get even with Miss Fatty Cat for all the thawumping.

We actually did have to set up a separate food and litter box area for Hiro because Samantha (aka "Miss Fatty Cat") would thawump her as often as she could. We called it "jumping the pooper" because it usually involved the end of a trip to the litter box. Hiro got smarter (and bigger), and Samantha got lazier, and they kept a happy distance from each other as adult cats.

Kimba did not seem to mind that Hiro was getting all of the writing attention for a while. As long as I played string with her a few times a week, she let us all live in peace.

Well, most of the time.

Kimba's special string was hidden in that drawer. They were hinting it might be time for a game.

Hiro and Kimba and her favorite string on their 6th
birthday. As a gift, I played until they were tired.
Hiro lost interest quickly.
Kimba lasted an hour.

GRATITUDE

As always, I could not have written and published this book without the support and nagging of my husband, Scott. He is the most important reader for every book I publish.

I am so grateful to Carol Hohle Communications for helping me transform my manuscripts for the first editions of the first two book in this series. Self-publishing is a terrifying process, and I am so thankful for the honest, trustworthy, and reliable people who help me fulfill my dreams. I adapted and took over the process myself, but I never would have started so smoothly without Carol's experience and guidance.

Special thanks to my mom for pulling her technical writing skills out of retirement to give everything one last look.

And I must add a note of thanks to all the children (and adults) who shared their love of my first book and urged me on to this second one. I hope you enjoyed it!

Thank you, Hiro, for always letting us know
exactly where we belong.

WORDS YOU MAY NOT KNOW

The teacher in me loves to throw fun words into my stories, but you may find that some of them are new to you. Here's a few from each chapter, just in case you need to check on what they mean in the story.

So Far In The Series

cohabitate: (verb) live alongside of or with

enlisted: (verb) enrolled, signed up, or joined in an activity or army

feline: (adj.) cat or cat-like

Chapter 1

condominium: (noun) a single unit or home that is part of a large building or apartment complex

engrossed: (verb) totally focused on or paying attention to one thing only

feral: (adj.) wild or untamed; going back to a wild status after having been tame or domesticated

feebly: (adv.) weak; lacking in volume or strength

Typhoon: (noun) a tropical storm, cyclone, or hurricane of the Pacific Ocean

Tsunami: (noun) an unusually large sea wave caused by an undersea earthquake (seaquake) or undersea volcanic eruption (note: T is silent)

traipsing: (verb) walking without solid direction or focus on reaching a goal; wandering

Chapter 2

hunkered: (verb) squatted on one's heels, back legs, or haunches; hunch down

niggled: (verb) tickling, poking, and demanding attention

pedicures: (noun) professional care of the feet, usually including trimming and painting of toe-nails

undergrowth: (noun) low plants or bushes, often beneath trees or larger plants; underbrush

Chapter 3

unauthorized: (adj.) without proper permission or paperwork; done in secret, without telling authorities or those in charge

venturing: (verb) daring or risking to go on a trip or adventure; risking harm on a dangerous trip

overreacting: (verb) to react or act more than is needed, called for, or appropriate

communal: (adj.) used or shared by everyone in a group; belonging to a whole community

destiny: (noun) a plan and sequence of events that cannot be avoided; something that will happen to an individual; lot or fortune

devious: (adj.) cunning, tricky, shifty, or untrustworthy

Chapter 4

radar-like: (adj.) moving carefully in order to capture sound, like an electronic radar system moves to pick up radio waves

dilemma: (noun) a problem involving a difficult choice, unusally unpleasant or unwelcome

abandoned: (verb) to leave completely and finally to never return; desert

Chapter 5

leisurely: (adv.) done slowly, calmly, without hurrying in any way

agitation: (noun) upset, restless, or annoyed state

rhythmically: (adv.) having a flowing beat and consistent rhythm, like a drum beat

perplexing: (adj.) confusing, unclear, or not understood; puzzling

"tip of the iceberg": (idiom) a small part of something much larger and unknown or unseen that is dangerous or can cause trouble; meaning comes from the fact that roughly 90% of an iceberg is below the surface and what can be seen from a boat is only the very tip of it

Chapter 6

din: (noun) a loud, confused, ongoing noise

swig: (noun) a big swallow or gulp of liquid

furrowing: (verb) making wrinkles in the face, especially forehead, by scrunching or frowning

oblivious: (adj.) unaware, clueless, not paying attention

ancestors: (noun) relatives who came before you in the family line, like a father or grandfather, but often meaning someone many generations earlier

Ice Age: (noun) The Ice Age began 2.4 million years ago and lasted until 11,500 years ago. During this time, the Earth's climate repeatedly changed between very cold periods, where glaciers covered large areas of the world, and very warm periods when many of the glaciers melted.

endangered: (adj.) threatened with danger; in this usage specifically animals in danger of becoming extinct because there are so few of them left on Earth

hospitable: (adj.) warm and welcoming; open and friendly to guests; in this usage referring to planets that would be open to the support of life with breathable air, water, and a food supply

Chapter 7

saunter: (verb) walk at a slow or leisurely gate, usually with attitude; amble or stroll

bottlebrush: (adj.) resembling a brush with stiff bristles surrounding a thin wire that is used to clean out narrow bottles

posture: (noun) position or way of holding the body

Chapter 8

vivid: (adj.) extremely realistic or lifelike; very intense and full of spirit; very clear and bright

surveillance: (noun) constant watch kept over a certain place or person, usually for the purpose of gaining information; ongoing record of the activities or a person or group

vigilance: (noun) watchfulness; alertness to danger or attack; wariness

fascinated: (verb) caught and held the attention or interest of someone; was special in a way that aroused the interest or curiosity of someone

Chapter 9

restored: (verb) put back in a place or a former position; given back or returned

portals: (noun) door, gate, or entrance; entrance to a tunnel, mine, or other location—in this case outer space or communication with the ship

frantic: (adj.) wild, crazy, or desperate

timid: (adj.) lacking in self-confidence, courage, or bravery; shy and hesitant; easily frightened

"more than she bargained for": (idiom) received an unexpected or unplanned outcome, usually because something bad happened; got a larger and worse outcome than expected or planned for

azure: (adj.) a light, clear shade of blue, like a summer sky

Chapter 10

tangible: (adj.) real items that can be touched and felt; not imaginary or visionary

democracy: (noun) form of government in which individuals vote and select their leaders, who then represent them directly; government ruled by the people it governs

vying: (verb) competing, fighting, or struggling for position or power

disgruntled: (adj.) angry, upset, or displeased; grouchy or grumpy

queasy: (adj.) sick or nauseous; having an upset stomach or bad feeling

vulnerable: (adj.) open to attack or harm; able to be hurt or wounded, even killed

Chapter 11

regal: (adj.) relating to a king or queen in beauty and poise; splendid or stately

sophisticated: (adj.) educated, cultured, worldly, and cultivated

contort: (verb) twist, bend, or force out of natural shape

telltale: (adj.) reveals or shows something that was supposed to remain hidden; tells the tale; gives warning or notice of something

Chapter 12

alarming: (adj.) causing fear, danger, or distress

edgy: (adj.) impatient, cranky, or jumpy; being "on edge" and grumpy

"bide his time": (idiom) wait for just the right time or opportunity; be patient and wait until the time is right to act on something

diligently: (adv.) constant effort to accomplish a goal or task; unwavering and hardworking focus on a task; persistently

console: (noun) part of a computer made up of the keyboard and switches that control the machine

obnoxious: (adj.) offensive, upsetting, annoying, rude, and generally objectionable in every way

upstart: (adj.) rising from humble beginnings to a position of power and authority; a desire to rise and gain power, position, and influence

ambitious: (adj.) eager or excited to gain power, position, wealth, and importance; seeking constantly to better oneself in society

moles: (noun) hidden spies; double agents; individuals who claim to support one side but are really gathering information for another; spies who are undercover or "underground," like a mole

Chapter 13

savoring: (verb) enjoying a smell, sensation, or moment and taking the time to really appreciate it; to relish or thoroughly enjoy a moment or thing

dignity: (noun) self-respect or worthiness; pride

essence: (noun) the basic, real, unchanging nature of a thing; the inward nature or true substance of a thing

undercover: (adj.) working out of sight, secretly, or in disguise

frayed: (verb) stressed, upset, worn out by fear, and strained to the point of snapping, like a rope can be worn away until it breaks

wary: (adj.) cautious, watchful, and on guard for danger

high-profile: (adj.) important or attracting a lot of attention; high on the list of those getting special treatment

taut: (adj.) high-strung, stressed, tense, or emotionally strained

Chapter 14

woozy: (adj.) confused, dizzy, faint, out of sorts, or slightly nauseous

boggled: (verb) overwhelmed, confused, and bewildered by an event or thing

expectantly: (adverb) expecting, anticipating, or waiting for something

sushi: (noun) form of Japanese cooking where rice and fish, vegetables, or other food items, sometimes raw, are rolled in a long piece of seaweed and then cut into bite-sized pieces

famished: (adj.) starving or extremely hungry; desperate for food

"out of line": (idiom) disagreeing with what is expected; not behaving in an expected and proper way

unnerving: (adj.) upsetting, flustering, or making one nervous; causing one to loose confidence or nerve

Chapter 15

solemn: (adj.) extremely serious, formal, or somber

bond: (noun) a formal or informal agreement that unites two individuals; a uniting or binding force

brazen: (adj.) shameless, bold, or disrespectful

Chapter 16

imperative: (adj.) urgent, vital, absolutely necessary

disruption: (noun) interruption, disorder, disturbance, or break in routine or normalcy

enduring: (verb) tolerating; allowing without resisting or fighting; suffering through something

mauled: (verb) attacked or given a rough beating to do harm; handled roughly

"window of opportunity": (idiom) perfect moment that should not be missed; time during which there is a chance to do something, like an open window allows for escape

Chapter 17

"be beside himself": (idiom) in a state of extreme excitement or happiness; "beside" used to mean "outside" of something, so the phrase meant so happy that a person felt out of their mind or outside of themselves, possibly even a bit crazy with glee

"feeling out of sorts": (idiom) somewhat ill or sick, but mostly just feeling not quite right or on top of things

"get her bearings": (idiom) to figure out one's position or get your feet solidly under you, literally or metaphorically, so one feels secure and in control; to gain some poise, calm, and control in a situation

factions: (noun) small groups within a larger group that hold themselves apart or separate for some reason or purpose; clique or group that keeps out others from a main group

sentimental: (adj.) full of love or strong positive feelings and tender emotions

Chapter 18

gawking: (verb) staring too long and intently; staring stupidly or awkwardly; gaping

Chapter 19

unkempt: (adj.) messy, not combed, neglected, or uncared for

aloof: (adj.) reserved, held back, disinterested, or kept at a distance

pathetic: (adj.) pitiful, sad, terribly unhappy or sorrowful

chortled: (verb) chuckled or laughed gleefully

Chapter 20

retching: (adj.) sounding like gagging, throwing up, or vomiting

industrious: (adj.) hardworking, diligent, and full of energy to complete a task

enticing: (adj.) causing strong attraction or interest

splayed: (verb) spread outward or extended at an especially awkward angle

ABOUT THE AUTHOR

Meg Dendler has considered herself a writer since she won a picture book contest in fifth grade and entertained her classmates with ongoing sequels for the rest of the year. Beginning serious work as a freelancer in the 1990s while teaching elementary and middle school, Meg has more than one hundred articles in print, including interviews with Kirk Douglas, Sylvester Stallone, and Dwayne "The Rock" Johnson. She has won contests with her short stories and poetry, along with multiple international awards for her best-selling "Cats in the Mirror" alien rescue cat children's book series. *Bianca: The Brave Frail and Delicate Princess* was named Best Juvenile Book of 2018 by the Oklahoma Writers' Federation.

Meg and her family live in Arkansas.

Visit her at www.megdendler.com for more information about upcoming books and events and all of Meg's social media links.

Lightning Source UK Ltd.
Milton Keynes UK
UKHW020328230219
337728UK00009B/707/P

9 781732 380684